The Marseille M

Kaya Quinsey

Dedication

For my family.

Copyright Page

The Marseille Millionaire

A Coco Rose Books Publication

Title page adapted from iStockphoto.com images

First e-book edition January 2020

www.kayaquinsey.com

Chapter One

On a chilly June morning, Elise pulled her blanket right up to her chin. She was unaware of the significance the day ahead carried.

After feeding Langdon, her cat, and making a pot of coffee, Elise sat on her living room sofa. Bleary-eyed, she watched the sailboats begin their journey from the harbor.

The first thing on her to-do list—track down Gerard Remieux. In the excitement of the moment, she missed his signature. She needed his signature on an important line of a sales document. They were closing on his house. Without it, the sale may as well never have happened. She never made these kinds of mistakes. But then again, she never made this kind of sale. As an eighty-something-year-old in their small town, it wasn't hard to guess Gerard's whereabouts. Options were minimal in Ashfield - a prosperous small town on the coast of the Atlantic. Especially for millionaires. And since Gerard didn't carry a cell phone, Elise's first stop would be the Ashfield Golf and Country Club.

She glanced up at the sound of rustling from the closed spare bedroom door. Her younger sister, Rose, emerged with her blonde hair piled on top of her head. Rose wore a floral-print kimono Elise didn't recognize. Something new she must have found at the flea market, Elise assumed.

"Do we have any Danishes?" Rose asked, a sleepy grin forming on her symmetrical face. For ages, Rose had been the world's easiest roommate (if you didn't count Langdon). Except for her complete inability to check for small items around the house. But recently, Rose had been acting like, well, a teenager. When Elise was Rose's age, she had been the same. So, she didn't blame her for it. But she struggled with whether she should or should not be setting curfews and boundaries... she wasn't Rose's mother, and she never would be.

Elise knew better than to answer Rose anymore, when she asked her those sorts of questions. She was doing her best to teach Rose as best she could. Rose walked into the kitchen herself, emerging with a cherry Danish. For years, Elise had done her best to be a mother figure to her six-years-younger sister. They had lost their parents in a car accident ten years earlier. While Elise had been twenty, Rose had only been fourteen. The trauma lay indelible, invisible scars on them both, but Elise knew it had been hardest on Rose.

"You know, your birthday is coming up," Rose said as crumbs fell onto the white leather sofa. Rose sat, perched like a cat, with her legs beneath her, as Langdon sprawled out in the morning sun. Elise checked her phone. Only ten minutes before she had to leave.

Elise took a deep breath. "Don't remind me." She drained the remnants of her coffee.

"And not only coming up, like in a long time. It's this weekend. It finally falls on a Saturday. Finally! We can celebrate! Maybe we should go out to that restaurant in town that just got a Michelin star – what's it called again?"

Rose's enthusiasm was usually infectious. But her birthday was something Elise had never enjoyed celebrating. Not that she ever said that out loud. But that Elise had spent the last five birthdays at the office spoke volumes.

"Voulian," Elise replied, beginning to apply her makeup in the nearby washroom. She knew all the restaurants in town. Their late father, a prominent restaurateur, had ensured that his only two children receive the finest culinary education. This had usually been by way of eating at the best restaurants. But Voulian had opened only a year earlier, and with her busy work schedule, it was one she had yet to try.

"Voulian." Rose repeated, typing the name into her phone. "Okay. I'll make us reservations. For three? Did you want to bring that guy you've been seeing? Charlie, was it?"

Elise winced, grateful Rose was far enough away to miss it. She hadn't yet told Rose that another relationship (if it even was a relationship) was over at the one-month mark. She blamed her demanding work schedule. He had blamed her for not making time. But how else was she supposed to afford Rose's expensive college tuition? She paid the mortgage on their two-bedroom plus den condominium. Adding to the cost, it was in a high-end neighborhood in Ashfield, an even higher-end coastal town. Without putting in the hours, how could she support a lifestyle she had become accustomed to and Rose dependant on?

She said none of that to Charlie. Elise preferred not to discuss the harder things in life. It was a flaw of hers; she knew. She didn't open up without reason.

But then, why should she? Elise didn't see the point of opening up to people if she didn't have to. It only led to heartache and an influx of memories. Besides, her story felt complicated. At least, it did to her.

When Elise's parents died, a few unpleasant facts came out of the woodwork. Especially when it came to the financials. For instance, Elise had always marveled at her father's impulsive restaurant purchases. He'd open one restaurant. And then another. Before long, he had a whole sleuth of staff and managers at his beck and call. He had write-ups about him in the paper. Like everyone else, Elise assumed that her family was prosperous. She had no reason to believe otherwise.

But death has an unfortunate ability to uncovering suspicions. Elise recalled with crystal clarity leaving the family accountant's office, no clue what she was going to say to Rose. They didn't have money, which she had believed her whole life up until that moment. No, they were in debt. Thinking back to that negative number made her sick to her stomach.

After that meeting with the accountant, Elise knew she had no choice. With a heavy heart, Elise had sold their family home. There was no other choice. The numbers spoke for themselves. The sale of their $2 million home in Ashfield covered several loans her father had taken out. Elise sold off four of the restaurants to pay off the outstanding debts. With the debts paid, the meagre residue of the estate went into the down-payment of their current condo. That left a small chunk of change left over for savings. It hadn't provided much leftover for the day-to-day expenses.

"Make the reservation for two. I've got to run, sweets. I'll catch up with you tonight," Elise said. She zipped up her go-to black dress, before grabbing her stainless-steel travel mug. She filled it to the top with fresh coffee and flung on her most comfortable sling backs.

Her brisk pace showed there was not enough time today for the usual chitchat. But she managed a friendly nod to Oliver, the long-serving doorman of her condo. From Ireland, he loved to share stories with her, she being his favorite resident – unless he said that to everyone. She strode out of the main door with a glance across the road toward the entrance to the marina. The water in the harbor shimmered, and the marina bustled as usual with gangly adolescents wearing crisp white polo shirts. Like she once did, they waited for their sailing instructors. The air smelled of sweet grass, Elise noticed, as she hopped into her Mercedes sedan. She convinced herself it was a necessary career expense a few years earlier. That was before she got promoted. Now, she was the regional real estate sales manager at Cotherington Realty. The engine purred as she drove the short distance toward the Ashfield Golf and Country Club.

Gerard Remieux was the eighty-something-year-old French millionaire she needed to track down. Somewhat of an oddity in their small town, he made himself at home in Ashfield for a few months every year. He alternated in what she imagined was a succession of mansions worldwide. Recently, she helped him sell his $4.2 million-dollar estate. At least, that's what she was trying to do. If she could only get that one last signature. It was no wonder that the mogul was popular with women. With a thick French accent, a deep tan, and a fishing empire behind him, he was a catch. Now, women at least half his age surrounded him, as she spotted him poolside. She waved to him as she parked, downed the last sip of coffee and signed for her visitor's pass.

As Elise approached, a scantily clad and cosmetically enhanced woman glowered at her from behind a margarita.

"*Bonjour* Monsieur Remieux. Aren't you looking well?" she called out in her best professional-yet-fun voice. Gerard turned to face her, his tan even deeper than yesterday. He walked over and gave her a hearty kiss – one on each cheek.

"*Bonjour* Elise. To what do I owe the pleasure of your company?" he asked, gripping her shoulders affectionately. The woman behind him glared at her even harder.

Elise whipped out the papers from her oversized purse. "Signatures. I do apologize," she added to him, as she laid them on a glass table. She had to be careful not to let the beads of pool water drip onto them. "I'm afraid we missed one." Elise fumbled to find a pen, but Gerard, suave as ever, pulled one from seemingly nowhere. A Montblanc, no less. After he finished signing with the flourish of his pen, Elise noticed her shoulders ease.

"*C'est tout*?" he asked her. That is all? As she nodded, the amount of her commission check finally set in. Gerard peered at her.

"And now, to celebrate!" Elise said, reaching for the bottle of champagne she brought with her. It was just after nine o'clock. But surely the club could offer orange juice.

Gerard's face lit up at the prospect of a morning mimosa. He waved a wait staff who returned with what they needed. Elise uncorked and poured their celebratory drinks. Excitement bubbled up in her almost as fast as the bubbles rising in her glass.

"Cheers!" she said, clinking her glass with his, and taking an appreciative sip. It was customary at the end of a big sale.

"You do many of these kinds of sales?" Gerard asked her with a dismissive wave of his hand. As if multimillion-dollar home sales was small potatoes. Perhaps to him, they were.

Elise smiled and nodded. "Yes. Not all the time. But we do a few every year."

Gerard's bushy eyebrows shot up. "We?"

"The firm. Cotherington Realty," she said in professional tones. She debated whether to tell him that this was, in fact, the first sale she made over two million dollars. Let alone four. Property sales were down pretty much everywhere, although she was doing well. Few real estate agents were making the big money these days. There weren't that many properties of that caliber in Ashfield.

He nodded, looking lost in thought. "I see. And you? You like this sort of work?"

Elise had gotten used to these sorts of questions at the end of a sales transaction. The conversation drifted towards this, to which she enthusiastically nodded. And they would, in turn, tell her a little about their work. It was all part of the closing process.

Gerard began to say something, but a staff member came to tell him he had a phone call. He looked at her apologetically.

"I am sorry to go. But glad to see you walk away? Is that the saying?" he said, the corners of his eyes forming deep creases as he smiled.

Elise laughed. "*Oui. Merci encore*," she added to him, and downed the last of her mimosa.

Back at the office, another party was underway.

"Here, here! To Elise, reigning in a new empire for Cotherington Realty!" Joe Cotherington, her boss, said as he clapped her on the back. The rest of their small team gave their approval through whoops and cheers. As another celebratory bottle of prosecco got passed around, Joe turned to her.

"You know, Elise, this sale has really brought our firm to a new level. I mean, I know we call ourselves a boutique luxury real estate firm, but truly..." he shook his head appreciatively. "...your professionalism on this one was out of the park. And the fact you speak French? That helped matters." He laughed his usual big, gregarious laugh. "I've got another French guy coming in this week who just called me before you walked in. Wants to buy a place on the port. You interested?"

Elise nodded in excitement.

"He's coming in tomorrow," Joe told her, checking his phone to confirm. "From a place in France I've never heard of. Maybe you have. Mersay? Or something like that?"

Chapter Two

The next morning, Elise woke up to her alarm and to an overheated condominium. Boiling, she peeled the blanket off and ran to the thermostat. After fiddling with it for a few moments, she let out a moan of frustration.

"Why's it so hot in here?" Rose asked in a tired voice.

Elise took a deep breath and counted to three before answering, doing her best to quell her irritation. "It seems like the thermostat broke. The heating system is on and won't shut off. I'll call the company," she said in crisp, even tones.

As Rose went to make the coffee, Elise punched in the phone number for the big box store that supplied and installed her thermostat less than one year ago. After being redirected a few times through the automated system, she let out a wail as they disconnected her, for the second time.

Rose walked over to the windows, opening every one of them as wide as they would go.

"Too bad this hadn't happened yesterday, when it was cold out, huh?" Rose said, as sticky, humid air from outside began to fill their home. "What are we going to do? I feel like we're being smoked out."

Elise stood frozen. The perspiration from her forehead leaked down into her eyes. In an instant, she whipped into action. "Okay. Forget the coffee. You grab Langdon, a water dish and his kibble, pick up your coffee from the corner and head to Nina's or any other friend's house with air conditioning for the afternoon. I'll get this mess sorted," she said with more conviction than she had. Today, she had a meeting with a new client. She couldn't show up looking like she came from a hot yoga class. A bead of sweat trickled down her back.

As Rose scrambled to get sorted, Elise did her best to collect herself. She called the mega-store again, eventually reaching someone from the servicing department who didn't put her on hold. Sorry, they said. With the hot summer weather, they were swamped and couldn't send anyone for at least two days. As nothing more could be done, they made an appointment, the problem as solved as it would be, and Elise breathed a sigh of relief. And then she got out of her unit. Stepping out of the elevator, she walked past the doorman who looked at her with some concern.

"Everything all right, Ms. Laird? You look like you just got back from a hard run or seen a ghost."

"Yes, Oliver, everything's fine. Thank you so much. Just dealing with a tricky thermostat in my unit. It's all taken care of."

At the Port Roastery, her favorite nearby coffee shop, Elise's phone was blowing up. For the next twenty minutes, she locked herself in the bathroom. She rinsed her face, drank her coffee, applied her make-up and fixed her hair. All the while, she fielded text messages from Joe.

The frenchie is in

I need you to meet him for lunch

Elise–this is big. Big. Big. BIG!

She didn't need Joe to tell her how important this was. She knew. The knots in her stomach said it all. After arranging a time with Joe – noon for lunch at Frakas, a family-run Greek restaurant near the Port–Joe would arrange it with the client's assistant.

Wait, she texted him. **What's his name?**

Luc Dubonier.

Elise grabbed her usual table at Frakas. Mary, the owner, was her usual self. She was still bussing tables at twice the speed of the bus boy they had hired. Otherwise, Mary was bossing around her husband, and making recommendations to customers about what was the best on the menu. Elise had already tried most of the dishes they had. Frakas was a favorite of hers. Well renovated, with everything outfitted in crisp sea-blue or white. With a bustling open kitchen, patrons could glimpse behind the scenes. Elise had been coming here since she was a little girl. Mary and Nico, the owners, had been close friends of her parents. They had been the pseudo aunt and uncle that she and Rose had leaned on that first year after that fatal day. And their pita bread and dips had a way of making the harsher edges of life feel a little fuzzier. Plus, the food was excellent and the owners charming. But her favorite thing right now about Frakas was that it was always over air-conditioned.

After retouching her makeup in the washroom, the harsh lighting making her feel like she might have over-applied her concealer, Elise now waited at a table for two. Her foot tapped at the chair leg. She always got like this before meeting a client. It was, in her mind, what kept her on her game. What kept her hungry. What kept her from using the same sales pitches, the same lines, the same hooks–time in and time out. She had seen it before happen to her colleagues, whose sales figures were respectable. But they hadn't come close to touching hers. No one's did.

She reviewed her notes on the most recent sales figures of Ashfield's real estate market. There were a lot of new listings and sales looked like they were picking up. And she had three, possibly four, properties to show to Luc. Or Mr. Dubonier. She didn't know how formal he was. With millionaire-types, you never could tell right off the bat.

His family owned a rather large-scale telecom company in Europe, according to Google. And as they seemed to hint from an interview she pulled up online, may expand into the American market. The photos were all old, nothing recent. Most of them featured Luc smiling for posed photos. One she found, in an undated magazine spread of him, a photo of his wife, and his teenage son. But again, these were from ten, fifteen years ago. So she was looking for a man much older than the one in the photos.

The bell chimed, signaling an incoming patron. With her head still spinning with sales data, Elise almost didn't notice. As she turned her head to check, she realized it wasn't him. The man at the door looking around was young. He was in his thirties–early forties tops. With dark brown hair, scruffy facial hair, and a rumpled white shirt, that surely wasn't him. She turned back to her phone, perusing through her Instagram account to pass the time.

"Elise?"

She looked up to see the disheveled man peering at her expectantly.

"Yes, can I help you?" she asked. She was used to people around town stopping to chat. But usually that was with people she knew. Not total strangers. She noticed his shirt, although wrinkled, was a fine linen dress shirt.

"I am Luc. Luc Dubonier," he said, with the slightest French-accent, hand outstretched. "I believe we had a meeting arranged?"

Elise's eyes widened. She gazed at him, taking him in.

He's too attractive to be my client, she thought before she could stop herself. He gave a lopsided grin, as if reading her mind. "Uh, yes. I'm sorry, you're Luc?" she asked him for clarification. As he nodded, she did her best to smooth her flustered feathers. "I–I'm so sorry. I saw you come in. I was looking for someone much, uh–" she fumbled.

"Older?" he suggested, a shy smile forming on his full lips.

Relieved, she nodded. As if reading her thoughts, he piped in. "My dad has the same name..." he said, trailing off. "This isn't the first time this has happened. I am technically, well, Luc Dubonier the second. Or third, if you count my grandfather..."

In his attempts to reassure her, Elise felt her cheeks hot with embarrassment. He pulled up the chair across from her, and settling down to work out the details, rolled up his linen sleeves past his elbows. As her eyes darted to his arms, something she always seemed to do with men, a tingle ran down her spine. They were tanned. Strong. Solid. Not that there was anything wrong with weak arms, she tried reminding herself. When was the last time she had been held by a man with strong arms? She shuddered that it had been that long.

"So," Elise began, trying her best to wipe the slate clean and regain some composure. "Luc. Tell me what you're after?" She pulled out a pen and notepad from her purse, ready to scribble. Foreign buyers were often specific. They knew what they wanted, where they wanted it, the square footage down to the inch. They had done as much, if not more, research into Ashfield than she had, or so they often thought, and were eager to get down to business right away.

But not Luc.

He picked up the menu in front of him, examining it as if he had never seen one before, hemming and hawing over what appetizers they should start with.

"The calamari here is excellent," she suggested. Over the sounds of sizzling coming from the kitchen, waiters called to one another back and forth. The hum of upbeat jazz played over the sound system.

He looked about ready to decide when Mary walked over with her characteristic ear-to-ear smile. She was used to Elise bringing business associates and clients to Frakas. But they were not young or good-looking. Mary did not appear to miss that.

"Well well," she began teasingly, a hand placed on one hip. "Looks like Elise here has finally brought a man of hers to my place. You know, it's always work for her–"

"Mary!" Elise chimed in, ready to burst from humiliation at any moment. "This is Luc. Luc Dubonier. He's come all the way from France to look for a property," she said through clenched teeth, a huge smile frozen on her face.

But Mary was Mary–unfazed and unabashed. "Pardon me," she said, bringing her hand to her mouth. "Well, I'll get out of your hair then. But, I would highly recommend the calamari. And the pita with the three dips. Just to start, of course," she added with a wink to Luc.

Elise shot Luc a grateful smile. He appeared bemused by the entire spectacle, and he beamed back at Mary.

"We will have one of each to start. And," he looked to Elise uncertainly. "You like white or red?"

Mary chimed in. "Wine at lunch. A man after my own heart!"

"I usually go for the white wine," Elise answered. She always stuck to her unofficial one-glass-at-lunch policy with clients.

"And one liter of your house white. *Merci*!" he added, the corner of his mouth twitching. As Mary left with the menus, Elise sat up a little straighter and did her best to retrieve her dignity.

"Now, we have some very nice properties at the moment down on the–" she began.

"But whyyyyyyyyyy?" the woman seated next to them wailed. Up until now, the duo beside them had been an inconspicuous couple. "You're breaking up with me?" Her voice rose to a higher pitch.

Elise cleared her throat, determined to continue. "—as I was saying. We have some gorgeous properties right now–"

"Is there someone else?" Now the woman's voice was rising. People's heads were turning. The man across from her shifted uncomfortably.

"—the port's property values have held up well the last few years despite the–"

"There is someone else! It's Lisa in marketing, isn't it?" the woman was full on yelling now. No one in the restaurant could focus on anything else, as the busy chatter of the restaurant died down and came to a halt. And as Elise turned to gauge Luc's reaction, it seemed he was enjoying the spectacle as much as everyone else.

"Babe, why don't we calm down and take this outside..." the man attempted, as he cast his gaze out to the restaurant, all whose eyes were on them.

"This is just like Montauk all over again, Steve! Don't tell me to calm down!" the woman snapped back at him. And the pair of them yelled non-stop as they worked their way to the exit. It wasn't until the door chime jingled as the door slammed shut that the usual clamber of the restaurant resumed.

Elise sat in silence for a moment, not sure if she should resume with her sales pitch, like nothing had happened. Luckily, she caught Luc's eye. And then she lost it. It started with a quick escape of a giggle. Then it turned to a quiet attempt at suppressing the laughter. Luc wasn't doing much better. A laugh escaped from Luc, and soon after the pair of them were clenching at their stomachs, gasping for air.

"I'm sorry, it's not funny..." Elise began wiping away at a tear.

"No, no. Not funny at all," Luc agreed, clearing his throat. "So, should we?"

As they were about to get down to business, Mary arrived with the liter of wine, calamari, pita bread, three dips, a basket of bread, and a flaming saganaki. On the house, she insisted.

Elise knew in that moment that nothing productive would be discussed over that lunch.

Elise was surprised when she checked her phone while Luc went to the washroom that a whole hour had passed. They had finished the liter of wine, enjoyed their main dishes (grilled salmon on a Greek salad for her, steak and Greek potatoes, rice, and a Greek salad for him), and were now waiting on the espresso. She had learned a few things about him over that hour. First, he was a talker. But even more–he was a sharer. He shared tid-bits of information with her. To Elise, he seemed out of character for the multi-millionaire son of a French telecom mogul. From where he went to school (La Sorbonne in Paris), to where he worked his first job (a restaurant in Marseille when he was fifteen–apparently his father wanted to teach him the value of hard work), being fired from his first job (kissing a waitress–the daughter of the owner of the restaurant), and what he did now (preparing to take over as CEO of their family company–Dubonier Enterprises).

The only thing they had yet to cover was why he was buying in Ashfield. It would have been an easy enough question to slip into the conversation, but Elise didn't want to rush him. She didn't want him to think she was a high-pressure, all-business sales person. Although a small part of her wondered if she was holding off because she enjoyed learning so much about him.

"A honey sponge cake, to share," Mary said as she placed the dessert down with a wink. "He's cute, honey. You should go for it!" Mary gave her a playful nudge.

"Mary, he's a client," Elise persisted. But she could feel her cheeks burning up. "Besides, you know my rule." She never dated clients. Elise couldn't help but glance at his unadorned left hand earlier.

Mary shrugged as she walked away while Luc returned.

"What did I miss?" he asked, his eyes bright and alert.

"Oh nothing," she said with a wave of her hand. "So, we should probably get down to–"

"You want to take a walk?" Luc said, gazing out the window. The way the sunlight dappled through the window, he looked like he could model for a sunglass catalogue. His sunglasses were tucked in his shirt pocket. Elise hesitated for a moment. Was this guy a serial killer? But then, a serial killer wouldn't make such a show of it, going through a real estate company and to lunch so publicly.

"Sure," she agreed after a moments hesitation.

He seemed to catch onto her hesitation. "There's a property. This beautiful spot. I would like you to tell me more about it," he explained. Elise nodded. She had grown up in Ashfield. And her entire professional career had been there. She knew all the hidden nooks and crannies of the town.

"Let's go."

They walked past the Port Roastery. Past the ice cream shop her parents took them to after every school recital. Past the sailing club in the harbor. Past the colonial-style Ashfield High School with its imposing columns and mile-high doors. The kind that made parents bend over backwards to get their kids into. As they walked in silence, into the adjacent neighborhood, Elise watched as Luc took it all in with wide eyes.

After about ten minutes of him guiding her down the wide, tree-lined street–a rarity since it was typically her doing the leading on these types of house tours–they stopped. Elise's heart pounded, dreading he would do as she had feared once they had turned onto Dalmatian Street.

"Here!" he said in delight. He held his hand out, like a friendly waiter, showcasing the stunning nineteenth century marble home with boxed hedges on either side of the gray wood door. There was a marble fountain in the middle of the circular driveway where a statue of a rabbit and a duck danced in the middle. It was all discreetly tucked away behind the high wrought-iron gate. "Slightly odd fountain choice," he remarked. "I mean, for such a classic home."

Her heart was going a mile a minute. Elise knew the names of those figures on the statue. Berta the bunny and Daffy the duck. She hadn't been that creative in naming them. After all, she had only been ten when her parents commissioned that statue. She had chosen a duck; Rose, a bunny. She stood in front of that manor for what felt like an eternity, taking it all in. She hadn't let herself look at the property in ten years. 1108 Dalmatian Street. And now that she was doing so, it was as she had feared.

Heart pounding. Head spinning. Knees weak. And considering her company, it was for all the wrong reasons.

"What's wrong?" Luc asked. Elise did her best to straighten up. Taking a deep breath, she exhaled, although it came out more as a shudder.

"I'm not sure it's for sale..." she began.

"That's where you come in!" Luc said in a resounding, ambitious voice. Elise's heart beat a little more quickly. What was he suggesting? That they ring the doorbell and offer the current owners a wildly inflated price?

But as Elise took a moment to think about it, she realized. This man could have a million dollars to spend, or five hundred million. She had no idea. She turned to him, suddenly all business.

"How much are you willing to spend?" she asked him, eyebrow cocked.

He smirked and crossed his arms. "One point six."

Elise scoffed. If there was one property that she knew in Ashfield like the back of her hand, it was this one. It had sold at the two million mark only ten years earlier, as they settled the estate. Elise had desperately wanted to keep it. But with paying off her parents debts, the maintenance of the estate, and the unexpected cost of the funeral, owning that home would never be possible. It had torn her heart to pieces, losing her parents and the family home in one fell swoop. But that was life, she reminded herself. And she had done a fantastic job at keeping herself distracted ever since.

Now, the closest thing she could get to that house again was to sell it at an inflated price to Luc. She wasn't going to tell him this was the house she grew up in. That afternoon had already been as far from professional as it got. And they were finally onto discussing business. She would not ruin her chance at another big sale. Besides, it would only open up the topic of her parents, which she was eager to avoid.

She crossed her arms and then re-crossed them. "You know as well as I do that's undervalued. If you want them to budge, you're going to have to wow them."

Twenty minutes later, Elise was walking up the familiar cobblestone driveway. Luc had left at her insistence. Truthfully told, Elise hadn't been sure she would make it to that front door. And she had not wanted him to bear witness–in case she chickened out or something. She passed by the birdbath; the one she would fill every summer morning with fresh water. The tree that her father had planted when she was born, and the smaller, wilder looking one beside it when Rose came along six years later. The fragmented memories, brought out by the smallest of reminders, were too much. By the time Elise got to the oversized double-door, she felt sick.

Ding-dong.

Even the sound of that familiar doorbell sent a shiver through her entire body that lingered as it ran down her spine. She rang the doorbell a second time, relieved when she was answered only by silence. She turned on her heel too soon, counting herself lucky, when the door swung open.

"Are you my new nanny?"

Staring up at her was a girl with pigtails tied in bows, a white flouncy skirt, and a green lollypop in her hand. She must have been three, four at the oldest.

"Uh, no–is your mommy or daddy home?" Elise asked the toddler. Fat tears began to well up in the little girl's eyes. Oh no. No no no no. Before she could say anything, there was the fast-paced clip clop of high heels on marble.

"Shayna, what did I tell you about opening the door?" the woman, whose heels had been clip clopping, scolded her daughter. "Now, why don't you go finish up with that cartoon you like."

Her daughter agreed, all signs of sadness having disappeared, as she skipped merrily to watch TV. As soon as the daughter was out of earshot, the woman's eyes whipped to Elise. "Can I help you?" she asked. Now that Elise had time to look at her more closely, she had dark circles under her eyes and papery skin that made her want to suggest a good moisturizer. But this wasn't about that.

Elise smoothed her skirt before holding out her hand. "I'm terribly sorry to bother you. My name is Elise. Elise Laird. I'm a realtor at Cotherington Realty. You might know us from our office downtown–"

"—Look, you seem like a nice person," the woman broke in. "But I'm really busy. My nanny just quit, I'm a single mom, I don't have time for sales pitches," she said. As her phone began to ring, she glanced at the number before she turned to Elise. "I'm going to take this. Nice to meet you, but I'm sorry, no to whatever you're selling."

And with that, the door closed in her face.

It took Elise a moment to recover. She could either knock again, at the risk of the police being called, or walk away, unsure of what she would tell Luc. As she rummaged through her purse for her phone, her hand brushed up again her notepad. Hang on a moment, Elise thought, as she grabbed her pen and began scribbling down her sales pitch. If she couldn't tell it to her face-to-face, this was the best she could do.

She folded up the letter she had written and put it in the mailbox, along with her business card. Walking off of that property, she kept her gaze steered towards the gate like a horse with blinders. The last thing this day needed was her collapsing into pieces at the sight of all these memories. She made it off of Dalmatian Street with even less conviction that she had come with.

Back at her condo that evening, Elise was burning up. Literary and figuratively.

Can I show you more properties? she texted Luc pleadingly, with whom she had loosely been in contact with since her failed meeting. It would make things so much easier for her if he would just look at another house. There were tons she could think of off the top of her head that he might have liked. But none of them compared to that home on Dalmatian Street.

Give it 24-hours, he texted back.

She turned off her ringer and put her phone in her purse. Elise took the damp cloth that she was using to keep herself cool and placed it over her eyes, feeling her tension melting into her sofa. The day's events kept replaying in her head. How had it gone so unexpectedly? Never in a million years could she have predicted the series of events that occurred. Luc was a change of pace from her usual buyers. A little thrill ran through her thinking about him. She heard the soft vibration of her phone rattling against her keys. Making a decision, she looked. She couldn't have expected the text she received, not in a million years.

What are you doing tonight?

Elise looked at Luc's text, sure she was reading into it. Still, her cheeks felt flushed as she re-read it for clarity. Certainly, he wanted to know if she was spending her time going over paperwork. He obviously wanted her to show him she was the best realtor Ashfield had to offer. Then came the next message.

Want to grab a drink?

There was no room for interpretation in that message. Her eyes widened, and she felt a swooping feeling in her stomach as she looked at her phone in awe. That was a universal phrase–she was sure they said it in French back in his home country as often as men in Ashfield. But was he asking her out? What did this mean?

Oh, who was she kidding? She knew this would happen the moment he walked over to her table. Elise's pulse quickened as she typed back.

Do you have a place in mind?

Chapter Three

Elise waited at The Oxblood. Popular and crowded, the club was packed with an eclectic mix of those in their early twenties and cougars out for a night of dancing. From the looks of the leopard-printed dresses surrounding the bar, the latter dominated the scene that evening. Rose had mentioned to Elise that this bar was the newest in town. She craned her neck to scan the crowd. So far, no sign of Luc. She had arrived ten minutes early, and he was now ten minutes late. But she had expected some nerves, which was why she had allowed herself a pre-date drink. It had escalated to three. Elise was feeling good.

On the Uber-ride over, she had convinced herself that this was simply a business drink. Like how she grabbed drinks with other realtors at the office. Or Joe, at the end of a long day. And the occasional large sale that deserved a celebration dinner. Come to think of it, it had been a long time since she had grabbed drinks with anyone outside of the office. As she checked her phone to distract herself one last time, she heard a familiar voice.

"Eleeeeese!" She flicked her head up to see Gerard, the eighty-year-old French millionaire, walking towards her. If walking was the right word. He seemed to have a certain bounce in his step. Was he shimmying? It looked like he was celebrating and enjoying the company of the women who looked on. She smiled as he arrived at her seat at the bar, giving him a peck on each cheek like she expected they did in France. He grabbed her arm to steady himself. From the glazed look in his eyes, it looked like he had been celebrating a lot. "You have met Luc, I presume?" he asked, gesturing behind him. Out of nowhere popped Luc, dressed this time in a pressed blue dress shirt and combed hair. A stark contrast to his disheveled appearance hours earlier.

This surprised Elise but she did her best to cover it up with a smile. "Yes, we have." She did her best to ignore the fluttering sensation in her chest as Luc lifted her hand to kiss. It was a move only very few men could pull off. Luc was one of them. "So you two know each other?" she asked, turning from one man to the other. Gerard threw back his head and erupted into peels of laughter.

"*Oui*. Yes, Elise. He is my Godson. You didn't know?" Gerard asked. Elise shook her head and cast a sideways glance at Luc, who appeared to be pretending to look elsewhere. "Of course, you should thank me," Gerard continued. "I spoke about you to him, and of course, now here he is! Took his private jet straight here and everything," he said conspiratorially. "Where were you coming from anyway? The Maldives? Venice?" he asked Luc, who shrugged in response with a sheepish grin.

After Gerard excused himself to buy a woman with long fingernails a drink at the bar, it was now Luc's turn to size up Elise.

"Be honest, you hang out at bars looking to chat up French men?" he teased. Elise felt the blood rushing to her cheeks. She hadn't expected him to turn up with Gerard. But now that he had, she actually felt grateful. Something, or someone, to talk about.

"Oh, you know. I'm a big hit with the seventy-plus crowd," she responded deadpan, before pulling a face.

He returned a wide smile. She hadn't realized how white his teeth were. They looked almost fake in the dim lighting, contrasting with his tanned skin. He gestured towards an empty table where she gratefully took a seat. She hadn't worn heels that high in ages, and her feet were already killing her.

"Miss Laird, tell me... are you really the best real estate agent in this town?" he asked her as he slid into his seat, eyebrow cocked.

Elise smiled back, taking the bait. "Well, if you define the best as the highest number of sales at the highest prices, then yeah," she responded cockily. She liked the way it sounded, bragging to him. He didn't flinch, or seem intimidated by her success, which was a huge hit in her books. On dates, not that this was one she reminded herself, she toned down her professional accomplishments.

After he flagged down a waitress, all wearing the same color as the name of the bar, and ordered a new round of drinks. Elise dove into a question she had wanted to know since they stepped onto Dalmatian Street.

"Why do you want that house anyway? There are tons of others nice houses in town. Many that are actually on the market."

He finished off his beer and faced her. "Elise, you know as well as I do that there are no other houses in town that compare. The columns, the acreage, the pond it backs onto, the privacy..."

Elise knew. She nodded in silent agreement. "I can understand that."

Two shots, a golden amber, arrived at their table, and there was Gerard lifting his drink in their direction. Luc raised an eyebrow.

"I will if you do?" he asked and downed his before she had time to respond. Elise couldn't remember the last time she had done shots. When she passed her real estate licensing examination? But even then, she had stuck to white wine. She put the shot glass to her lips and took a cautious sip. It tasted like cinnamon-hearts, and it left a warming feeling inside.

"Now, enough talk. This song rocks." Luc surprised her as he grabbed her hand from across the table. He pulled her towards the crowded dance floor with a live DJ playing some song she didn't know. It sounded like the music Rose listened to. She allowed herself to be led towards the music with a smile. It didn't escape her that this wasn't how she celebrated with clients. But then again, he was French. Was this customary? Gerard lifted his drink to them as they passed him. Before she knew it, she was on the dance floor. She was dancing to a song she didn't know, with a man she was almost certain she shouldn't have been dancing with.

Luc looked comfortable on the dance floor. He didn't grab at her or do any weird moves, only taking her hand to twirl her around. The sound of the bass flowed through her body, vibrating through her as she swayed along to the beat. Luc was a better dancer than her, but she didn't feel self-conscious, like she normally did on the dance floor. She felt his eyes on her, making her whole body tingle with excitement. She hadn't remembered the last time she had gone dancing. Let alone with someone who looked like him. Or looked at her like that.

Swaying from one foot to the next, she did her best to remain on the beat. But not Luc. A flick of his hand, a swivel of his feet—he was one with the music. She loved watching him move, like there was nothing else in the world that mattered. The dance floor got even more crowded as the music became louder.

This day and evening was unorthodox. A creeping feeling came over her, and she did little to fight it. As she caught glimpses of him looking at her, it was only strengthened. He smiled and the multi-colored lights hit his face, leaving him in a cavalcade of colors. He drew her closer. She could smell his sweat, his cologne. He sensed her easing up and ran his hand up her arm and down again, before spinning her. She knew he wanted the same thing that she did. Her heart skipped a beat as she made her move.

"Do you want to come over?" Elise whispered in his ear, in a moment of the heart winning over her head. If she had any doubts, they were nullified when he bit his lip and smiled back to her. Sure, she was all-business at work, she thought. But she deserved a little fun, didn't she? Yes, she considered. She certainly did.

No more spinning. Now he took her hand in his, leading her off of the dance floor through the crowds. Elise felt a warm swell in her chest and liked the way her hand felt in his. This was so exciting, she thought. She never went to clubs. She never did shots. She never met handsome French men as clients, especially men who looked like Luc Dubonier. She'd never had a one-night-stand. But there was a first time for everything, she reminded herself, as she rode out her instincts.

Outside of the Oxblood, she took in a deep breath, feeling sobered by the fresh air. Almost immediately, as the music faded into the distance and the only sound was of their footsteps, a cold feeling spread over Elise. Her condominium was a few blocks away, and she didn't want to take an Uber in case it dampened the mood. Besides, everyone knew everyone in Ashfield. For all the good in Ashfield, it was a haven for gossip. She didn't want the Uber driver telling his sister, who would tell their aunt, who would tell Mary back at Frakas that Elise had a one-night stand. It wasn't worth it.

The two of them walked the few blocks to her condominium in silence. She cast a nervous glance in his direction. Unlike her, he appeared at ease, taking in their surroundings.

How can such a man be so nonchalant? Elise wondered.

She fiddled with her code at the condominium. Oliver, the doorman, was away from the front desk and making his rounds. The pair of them waited side by side as the elevator arrived. She could feel her heart beat through her entire body. Elise swore she could feel his heart beat too. Her cheeks, she could tell, had turned scarlet in anticipation. As they got off of the elevator and she unlocked her condominium door, she was hotter than she had ever been.

Well, until a wall of humid, warm air hit them.

"Whoa! It seems very odd to be running your heating during this weather," Luc exclaimed from the doorway. Elise ran inside and tried to pry the windows open further.

Shit, she thought. She had forgotten about the heating system. The mood had vanished in an instant, as she felt herself becoming panicked. She clasped her hand to her forehead, which was already perspiring with beads pooling at her hairline.

"I completely forgot–"

"Hang on a moment," Luc said. He stripped off his shirt, tossing it haphazardly onto the floor. He walked towards her thermostat, which was blinking away incomprehensibly. Elise watched in stunned silence from the window, taking in his tanned, toned body, and the sure, direct movements he made. She only realized that she was staring after he spoke up.

"You have a screwdriver?" he called over to her, eyes fixed to the thermostat.

Elise took off her heels, not wanting to scuff the hard wood. She ran into the kitchen, rummaged around her kitchen cabinet dubbed by Rose as the "everything drawer". An every-bit-in-one screwdriver was beside a mound of rubber bands, a few extra wine bottle openers from the dollar store, and tape.

"Got it!" she ran over to him, feeling her cheeks flushing further. As Luc fiddled away with the thermostat, she poured them two tall glasses of water with extra ice cubes. The beads of condensation forming on the outside of the glasses mimicked Luc's body, which she observed from her carpet. Her leather sofa would be too sticky to sit on at that moment.

Elise did her best to ignore the rattling thoughts repeating themselves in her brain–thoughts like: What are you doing? He's your client? You never have one-night stands! After what felt like an eternity, Luc finally turned around, rosy-cheeked and proud.

"Done," he said coolly, but Elise could hear the swell of pride in his tone. Almost as soon as he said it, the hot air streaming out of the vents was replaced with an icy blast. Like balm on sore skin, and she pressed herself up against a nearby vent.

"That feels so good. How did you know how to do that?" she said, breathing a sigh of relief, a sleepy smile forming on her mouth. She did her best to suppress a yawn. But Luc seemed to catch it. He checked his watch.

"Another one of those first jobs I had. But it's late, sleepy girl. I should get going," he said, fumbling with his shirt.

Elise jumped to her feet and walked towards him. "No! No, stay," she said, all the while cursing herself for sounding so desperate.

Luc laughed gently and walked towards her. Was this it? Her heart raced as he planted a kiss on her cheek. "Good night, Elise." He cupped her cheek in his hand for a moment, his fingers trailing down her arm, his fingers lingering on hers for a moment.

And with that, he stepped out of her condominium. She gave him a brief wave as she shut the door, feeling herself crumple with humiliation and self-loathing in that instant. She had been so close. Before her parents had died, her mother had given her some sage advice–one-night-stands never worked out as planned. Her mother had been right. Had Luc been completely turned off by her incompetence with the heater? Thought her yawn was a sign to leave? A million thoughts poured through her mind as she brushed her teeth. She faithfully washed her face and applied her serum, night cream, eye cream, and lash serum, and finally got into her comfiest pajamas. After a couple of minutes of wallowing in self-deprecation, her head hit the pillow. At least she was doing so in an air-conditioned condominium.

Chapter Four

Elise woke the next morning, her head pounding. Memories from the night before replayed in her mind as she buried her face in the pillow. Hips swaying. Drinks. More drinks. Her inviting him over. Had they almost kissed? His hand lingering on hers... she took comfort in the icy air from the vent before again shuddering at the memory. Not because it wasn't wonderful, which it was. But had he rejected her? And had she garbled her chances at that sale?

How embarrassing.

She did her best to put all thoughts of Luc out of her mind as she stumbled into the kitchen. She felt grateful that Rose was still at her friend's house with the cat, so she didn't have to explain herself. Glimpsing herself in the kitchen mirror, she felt even happier no one was there. There wasn't a single chance he was interested in her now.

Her usual coffee-and-a-Danish routine halted as she checked her phone. Three missed calls and a voice mail from a phone number she did not recognize. It was only eight o'clock on a Friday morning. If it hadn't been from a local area code, she would have assumed it was a telemarketer. Her interest piqued as she listened to the message.

...this is Sam. Samantha Beedling. From 1108 Dalmatian Street. You left me your card and a note. I am very interested in further discussion. If you could call me back...

She would let out a squeal of delight if her head wasn't pounding. Instead, she wrote the number and called back straightaway.

"Ms. Beedling? Yes, this is she... thrilled that you expressed interest... ten o'clock? Same place? I will be there."

Two short hours later, Elise stood in front of 1108 Dalmatian Street again for the second time in two days. It felt like a cruel joke, made even crueler by her worsening headache. Before arriving, she had popped an Advil and chugged a blue Gatorade. She smiled, realizing her college hangover remedy still worked. Standing there again, she took in the changes that the new owners had made.

To the untrained eye, they made few apparent changes, but she knew that house inside and out. They had painted the shutters bright white instead of that creamy shade her mom had loved. The edges of the hedges were softer. The new owners, less meticulous than her father, had spent less time worrying about the edge of the shrub.

As she walked up those familiar steps, she did her best to suppress the rapid-fire memories.

Ding Dong.

Samantha Beedling opened the door, this time looking more relaxed. With a big smile plastered on her face, she welcomed Elise.

"Nice to see you again, Elise. I apologize for my abruptness the last time we met. I'm sure you can imagine what it's like, being a single mom and all," she said, ushering Elise into the formal sitting room. Elise hung on to her potential client's every word while taking in all the changes. They painted the walls a deep burgundy, the furniture too small for the large space, and a strong air freshener scent permeated the air.

Elise nodded, as if she understood what being a single mom entailed, and sat down on one of the tiny couches. After bringing two cups of black coffee for them both, the two women sat across from one another.

"So, Ms. Beedling, how long have you owned the property?"

The woman swatted at the air. "Oh please, call me Sam. I've been here for, what's it been? Nine? Ten years?"

Elise nodded. "And you're interested in selling?"

Sam straightened, bristling. "Well, you know. It's a lot of house for just Shayna and I. And my family is down in Atlanta. We might be persuaded, if the price was right," Sam said, a glimmer in her eye. Elise had seen that glimmer before. It meant big bucks. This lady wasn't going anywhere without a lot of zeros behind her.

Elise whipped out her notepad and began making notes. "Six bedrooms?" she asked, as Sam nodded. "And, how many bathrooms again?"

"Four and half."

"Right," Elise nodded, scribbling it down. She understood that, but she didn't need the owner of the house to think she glossed over details. "We can get down to specifics later. I have a buyer. A very interested buyer. Who just adores this property."

"Does he have a family?" Sam asked, her eyebrow cocked. "Because I just wouldn't sell it to one person." Her face saddened. Sam's resolute eyes becoming glassy for just a moment.

Although surprised, Elise masked it. "I see. And why is that?" she prodded.

Sam shifted on that small chair and took a thoughtful sip of her coffee. "Well, I don't know. This house..." she looked around, transfixed. "...it's just gorgeous. After my ex and I divorced a few years back, I don't know. It sounds silly, but... I thought I would have it all, you know? The big house, the perfect family... I'd like it to at least have another family. It did us well, at least for those few years we were here together," Sam smiled, but it didn't reach her eyes.

Elise nodded, captivated by the rawness that Sam displayed. She wouldn't peg her for sentimental.

Sam continued. "When we bought this place all those years back. I thought this was it. The perfect house, the perfect husband... I just feel like we failed to live up to it," she said, laughing. "I love this house. It's been a good home to us. I just want to do it right."

Elise nodded, touched by the sentiment. She did her best to fight the urge to well up with tears herself. This house had seen a lot. She would not give up that easily.

"I'll see what I can find out," she said, before changing the subject. She put on her best sales-smile and crossed her hands in her lap. "Now, when you move to Atlanta, how can I help you find the home of your dreams?"

Later that morning, Elise arrived home to find her sister's sandals back in their usual spot in the middle of the entrance, and a bag of kibble on the counter. Sitting on her bed beside a content kitty, Elise typed the message. She counted to three before pressing send, burying her face in her pillow and letting out a wail. Langdon leaped off of the bed.

"Look at what you've done. You've scared my poor baby," Rose said. Rose walked into her bedroom without knocking all the time. Now she carried Langdon like a baby. Langdon appeared none the worse for it, purring. Rose flopped onto Elise's bed beside her. "What's wrong with you?"

Elise looked down at the text message she sent Luc. If she ruined her chances with him, for whatever reason, then at least she could try to salvage some professional dignity.

Good morning–met with the owner of the house. I've got a good feeling. One small problem though.

She waited on bated breath. Then she heard her phone ping back almost immediately.

Good morning :-) -What's that?

A smiley face. Her heart skipped a beat. Why did he have to be so friendly? It made it hard to tame her feelings. She took a deep breath before she typed out her text, revised it, and pressed send.

The seller only wants to sell it to a family. She wants a family to grow up in that house.

So, what's the problem? I have a family, he replied.

Elise's heart dropped into her stomach as she stared at the text and re-read it to clarify. He has a family? Had she almost broken up a marriage? She felt sick at the thought. Why had he even agreed to come to her house? Before she could go into full panic mode, he texted back a picture of him and a golden cocker spaniel.

This is me and Joie. The perfect family :-)

Elise laughed and cursed herself for the relief when she got that picture. So, no family. No wife. And, she would have pegged him as a cat-person. Interesting.

Sure, Elise could tell Sam that the seller had a family. Lying wasn't out of the question–or as she liked to call it in sales, stretching the truth. But this house was different. It tugged at her heart in a way no other property could. And, she didn't want to taint this sale with manipulative tactics.

I have an idea, he wrote. **Set up an appointment for tomorrow afternoon.**

Elise thought better of asking his idea. Texting him was pushing at a sore spot. It took all her willpower not to send him some prideless text message, asking him why he went home the night before, anyway. It would appall some of her girlfriends. Or worst, ghosted him afterwards. But she wouldn't do that. She needed to work with him. Even if she didn't want to work with him, there was still her professional integrity. She didn't want to risk that–years of hard work had gone into building her reputation. With her pride barely intact, she didn't want to risk sending him yet another text message. Even if he was her client. So she let things rest, and set up that appointment.

The rest of the day was hazy and slow. Elise showed two mid-range homes to prospective buyers. She stopped by a discount furniture shop in the outskirts of town to buy some home accessories before staging some homes she would be showing. Glitzy mirrors, geometric print rugs... if it was Instagrammable, or even better–Pinterest worthy–it was in the homes she sold.

It was Friday night. She had dinner plans with Rose at La Bernadette—a French restaurant, popular with the locals. It was tucked away from tourists on one of the smaller streets that Ashfield had. It had an impeccable reputation and even better steak frites.

Her high heels clicked against the sidewalk as she made her way, certain that she would wait alone at the table for at least ten minutes. It surprised her to find Rose was already there. Rose gave her a little wave, and Elise greeted the waiter before she took a seat on the sleek white and chrome chair across from her.

"My, don't you look festive!" Elise said. She examined Rose's turquoise wrap top, her braided hair piled onto her head, and her gold dangling earrings. Their styles could not be more different if they tried.

Rose beamed at her. "You think? I got these today after class," she said, touching the earrings.

"How's that going, by the way?" Elise asked, scanning the wine menu. It had been awhile since she had caught up with her sister. Their schedules had been at odds for the past few weeks. With the chaos of the heating disaster, they had not had their usual time together.

Rose shrugged. Elise understood that shrug. That shrug that had quit the sailing lessons after one try. It was that shrug that had turned down prospective dates who got too close. It was that shrug she had done when she asked her if she was okay, months after her parents' death. Spoiler: she wasn't.

"What's wrong?" Elise prodded, while deciding on the Napa white Zinfandel. She watched as Rose, not one to stay silent, shifted in her seat. Elise knew Rose wasn't loving one of her marketing courses at university. Was she about to drop out? Her brow furrowed. "Seriously, what's up?" After a pause, "Hey, you can talk to me." When she thought Rose might crack, they were interrupted.

"Excuse me, ladies, can I offer you a bread basket? And, have we made a choice about the wine this evening?"

Elise ordered and tried to redirect her focus to Rose, who gnawed on a bread stick, averting eye contact.

"I think I will get the rosemary chicken..." Rose said, perusing the menu. Elise knew that Rose always got the Waldorf salad at La Bernadette. This was a stalling tactic.

"Out with it!" she nearly shrieked, so that a few heads from nearby tables turned. Rose's face turned serious.

"I need money," Rose said, avoiding Elise's stern gaze.

Too surprised to answer, Elise took a moment to respond. She thought Rose wanted to tell her she was dropping out of school–the final year of her liberal arts degree at Ashfield College. "You need money?" she echoed. Rose nodded, burning a hole in the table with her gaze. "How much?"

After what seemed like an eternity of silence, Rose spoke up. "Two fifty," she said at a barely audible volume.

Elise's fear vanished as a wave of relief poured over her. "Two fifty?" she repeated with a laugh. "Yeah, sure. I think I have it here in my purse. That's no–"

"No," Rose said with urgency. "Not two-hundred and fifty dollars." Her voice dropped a few notches. "Two-hundred and fifty thousand. Two-hundred and fifty thousand dollars."

Elise felt like someone had punched her in the gut, with no air to breathe. Rose liked to tease, but this was no joke. It was written all over her face. Elise's heart pounded through her chest, and the wine could not come a moment too soon. As their waiter poured a small amount into her glass to taste, Elise hurried him.

"That's fine, I'm sure. You can fill it up," she said with a fake smile, taking a large swig before Rose's glass was even full. It wasn't until she was three quarters of the way through her glass that she could string another sentence together.

"What happened, Rose?" she asked, her little sister's eyes welling with tears across from her.

Tears fell from her sister's eyes like fat raindrops. She could tell Rose was doing her best to rein it in. "Well, you know I love fashion. Obviously you know. And I've been so bored in class. I feel like I'm not learning anything. You know?" Rose gushed, the words tumbling out of her mouth. "And I went to this career fair that was being held at the school. One guy at a booth was cute. So I went up to him and we started to chat. Anyway, he worked at a bank. I had never heard of it before. Leighton-Long Credit Union. And he told me with my interest in fashion and the idea for the clothing store I had–"

"Your what?" Elise interrupted.

"My idea for a clothing store. For eccentric fashion in Ashfield. There's totally a market for it," Rose said, eyes wide and panicked. "He checked to see if I would qualify for a loan. And I did. I qualified on the spot, he said. It all happened so fast. We signed the papers, I was really pumped about the new business venture, and he said we could go over the terms later. But then this morning I got this in the mail." Rose pulled out a letter with trembling fingers from her purse. "Saying that I owe interest on the loan. Starting now. And I haven't been able to find a spot for the store, I haven't sold any inventory, and I don't know what to do. I don't know the first thing about starting a store," she wailed.

Elise felt lightheaded, trying to piece together everything her sister had told her.

"Where's the money now?" she asked her sister with an intensity that seemed to scare even Rose.

Rose paused for a moment before answering "Inventory," she said meekly.

"You already spent it?"

Rose nodded. "There is this Bangladesh-based wholesaler whose items are supposed to be selling at huge margins–"

Elise put her head in her hands, trying to take even breaths. "Jesus Rose. What the hell were you thinking?" she couldn't help herself from saying. "How on earth did you convince a credit union to lend you that kind of money?"

The waiter arrived to take their orders and looked at the pair of them. Realizing this was a bad moment, he walked away. Elise finished her wine before pouring herself a generous second glass.

"I knew you would never go for it, so I wrote your signature as co-signer."

Elise stopped breathing for a second. She picked up her glass of wine and downed it.

"So, to clarify. You forged my signature without my permission? You took out a two-hundred and fifty thousand dollar loan for a clothing store you only just thought of? And you used how much of that money on inventory?"

Rose looked panicked as she took a big breath before answering. "All of it."

"All of it? So you have nothing left?"

Rose blinked back at her before exploding. "Jimmy Clarkson told me about how so many people start successful businesses. I just thought–"

"Hold on," Elise said, breaking in. "Can't you sell it back to the original seller? Where is all this clothing?"

"I–I guess I should have done more research," Rose fumbled over her words. "They don't take returns. And, um, it's in a storage unit I rented. I owe them some money too."

Elise put her now throbbing head in her hands and thought hard. How could all this happened right under her nose? Hadn't she taught Rose better? Wasn't she a better role model than this? And an even bigger question, which she pushed out of her mind–what were they going to do to fix this?

Chapter Five

Elise had quickly asked for the check and left after Rose had dropped the bomb. Besides, Elise was in a storm of anxiety. She wondered if they could even afford the nice bottle of wine they had ordered. It would have to be a peanut butter sandwich when they got home. If she could even eat at all. She still felt queasy from shock.

"Are you mad at me?" Rose asked her for the millionth time as they walked back to her condo. Elise responded with silence. Not because she meant to cause her sister agony, which she was sure she was. She didn't know what to say. Yes, she was mad. But she was also mad at herself for somehow allowing this to happen in front of her. And she was furious with that bank-guy who never contacted her and had approved her little sister for a loan. With all that anger fuming and bottling up, she didn't want to explode. Best to stay silent, she told herself.

"Fine," Rose moped. "If you won't talk to me, maybe I'll go stay at Nina's house again tonight."

Elise exhaled as she fiddled with the lock, swinging open the front door. "You know, Rose. It seems like you will do what you want to do. So go do it."

Rose's eyes flashed with hurt. She collected her things in silence and left, leaving even greater quietness behind. Elise flopped onto her couch and felt like crying. She could feel the pressure building inside of her. The tightness in her chest. The heat radiating up to her cheeks. The prickling feeling in her nose. She hadn't cried since their parents' funeral. She had to be strong for Rose, she had told herself.

Well, look how well that had worked out.

Elise slept that night dreaming of running from a debt collector. He wore an old-fashioned suit and looking like the cartoon man with the monocle on the Monopoly box. Elise was trying to hide Rose away. But they were found. And she awoke the next morning, feeling unrested, to the sound of her alarm which was blaring away.

Elise felt restless all morning. Although she had applied extra concealer to mask her sleep deprivation, her yawning every ten minutes gave it away.

After she had shown a newlywed couple a prospective house, she was walking to grab yet another cup of coffee when she got a text message.

Hi Elise, it's Samantha (from Dalmatian Street)–is that client you mentioned still interested in the house?

Elise noticed that Sam was now using her full name. Sam meant business and Elise typed back. **Absolutely.**

I know it's unconventional, but I'd like to meet with the family before going ahead with any sale or negotiations.

Elise felt her heart sink into her stomach. As if the day wasn't going terribly enough. And it hadn't escaped her that the commission from this sale could help fix the difficulties that Rose had gotten herself into. Not that she wanted to fix the problem and let Rose off of the hook, but it would be nice to have the option. Now that the circumstances had changed, Elise felt determined to get that sale. Family or no family. She picked up her phone, brushing her pride aside, and gave Luc a call. As soon as he picked up she dove straight in.

"The seller wants to meet with you. Can you wrangle up a family?" she asked, only half-serious.

"Good morning to you too," Luc replied and yawned. Elise surprised herself as she felt a fluttering feeling in her chest when he spoke. She imagined him, lying in bed, his tanned chest peaking out from beneath crisp white sheets. She had to snap her attention back to the present to avoid her imagination from going south.

"So, can you do it?" she asked him, a hint of urgency creeping into her tone.

Luc paused, perhaps what he thought was a thoughtful pause, but to Elise was agonizing. "Yes. I can do that."

Elise exhaled a sigh of relief. "Okay. Fantastic. Well, why don't you and that family meet me at two o'clock at the house and you all can meet with Samantha yourselves."

"*Parfait. Merci Elise*," he replied before hanging up. Elise was left with an empty feeling in her stomach. Wolfing down two more danishes did nothing to quell that sensation.

The morning passed quickly. She showed one house to a taciturn buyer. To expend some nervous energy, Elise walked and walked until she was standing on the road in front of her old family home on Dalmatian Street. The butterflies kicked in. Thinking about her actions, she thought she should have felt like a cowboy–taking back what was theirs. The desire. The need. But she felt something closer to desperation.

I need this sale, she thought, as a black Mercedes sedan pulled up beside her. The front window rolled down, showcasing Luc in all his glory. He looked relaxed, like he might pick her up to go to the beach. Not like he was about to lock down a house with a fake family.

Speaking of, where was his fake family?

"Luc, where is your 'wife'?" she asked using air quotes. She was too worried that he was alone to worry about what he thought of her. But the sight of him sent a tingling feeling from the depths of her stomach to her fingertips.

If there was one thing Sam had been specific about, it had been that she would only sell to a family. And sure, a husband and wife was a small family, but it was still a family. Anyone but him alone.

Luc looked back at her, an amused grin forming on his face. "I am looking at her."

Elise's heart pounded as she pressed the doorbell. "I can't believe you wrangled me into this," she hissed at him. "This has got to be the most unethic—"

She was interrupted as the front door opened with Sam radiating a large smile. When Sam saw it was just the two of them, her smile wavered. But she regained her composure and extended a manicured hand to Luc.

"I'm Samantha. Samantha Beedling. Sam for you. You must be Mr. Dubonier?"

Luc matched her smile and shook her hand. "Please, call me Luc."

Elise didn't miss the quick glance Sam did, checking to see if there was anyone else in the driveway. If Sam was off-put, she hid it well.

"Come in," she extended her arm to the formal living room, where Elise had first sat. "Please, sit."

Elise once again found herself on the uncomfortably small seat. Luc looked huge by comparison as he perched on the corner of the chair. Even he seemed to notice that at any moment, that antique-looking chair could collapse under his weight. His curious eyes darted around the room.

That's right, it dawned on Elise. He hasn't been inside yet. From the way his eyes crinkled and the corners of his mouth were drawn up a millimeter, she knew it impressed him.

"Your home is spectacular," Luc said, observing the crown molding and chandelier.

"Thank you," Sam replied, looking flushed. "Now, is your family joining us today before the tour?"

There was an uncomfortable silence as Luc stood up and walked over to Elise, sitting beside her. She could smell his aftershave–woody and dry. He put an arm around her and gave her a gentle squeeze.

"This here is my family. My wonderful lady. My queen," he said with a huge smile. Elise knew he was trying to convey that they were an item, in love, though she wanted to thwart any and all questions before they emerged. Was Sam going to buy any of this? To her surprise, Sam beamed back at them in awe.

Sam's eyes bulged. "You two?" She pointed to the pair of them, looking for signs they were joking.

Elise jumped in. "I'm sorry I wasn't more forthcoming that the house was for my beloved..." she said, cringing at her use of the word 'beloved' as it spilled out of her. "... but he only just asked me to move in with him. Isn't that right?" She stroked his back, the way she imagined happy couples did. Every nerve ending in her body felt aware. His body seemed the same, as his shoulder muscles twitched.

Now was the moment of truth. Was Sam going to buy any of it?

The silence as Sam took in the pair of them was agonizing.

"Well, I knew something was up with you two since the second I opened the door," Sam replied, looking satisfied. "I have a knack for these things, you know. I've set up three of my cousins and my brother with their respective spouses. Not a divorce yet. Just mine," she said with a laugh. "But I have good sense for how other couples fare. You two are very much in love."

Elise did her best to make her smile look genuine, but inside she wanted to melt. This was too much! Luc would surely be scared away. She turned to check on his expression, sure that it would reveal the extent of how freaked he was. He was staring at her instead, his curious eyes giving nothing away. She could feel the skin on her neck prickling. Elise averted her gaze.

"So, shall we get started on that tour?" Elise piped in.

Two full hours had passed before Luc and Sam were acting like old friends. Elise doing her best to maintain an air of professionalism.

"Well, we love it," she said, turning to Luc, who nodded. "We are prepared to draft up paperwork and make you a very generous offer. In Luc's name." The three of them stood outside in the garden. The wooden playhouse her father had built for her was gone and replaced with a cheap plastic one, and the garden had been landscaped. Her mother had been fond of wilder gardens, allowing in whatever wanted to grow.

Sam shifted. "As this house isn't technically on the market, I'm afraid it won't come at a bargain."

Luc jumped in. "That's fine. I am–I mean we are prepared to negotiate."

"Four mill."

"Done," Luc said, extending his hand towards Sam, who shook it with vigor. Elise was horrified. Luc had overpaid by at least a million dollars of what the house was worth. She could have negotiated. She could have brought the price down. Who was this guy and how rich was he?

He seemed unfazed by the gross overpayment and Elise's horror. His eyes shone as he talked in wild excitement about the house with Sam. This continued as they walked back through the house towards the entrance. Elise and Luc said their goodbyes to a thrilled looking Sam, and Elise promised to have the paperwork sent over by courier later that afternoon.

As the door swung shut behind them with a heavy thud, Luc ran over to Elise and picked her up, twirling her around. Placing her hands on his broad shoulders to steady herself, she had never had this kind of response from a client. Especially not from a client who had wildly overpaid. As he put her down, his face was the textbook definition of joy.

"You did it!" he said, shaking his head in shock.

Elise smiled, feeling a warm swell in her chest, and gave a humble shrug. "We did it. This was all your idea. I just helped bridge the gap."

Luc shook his head. Elise realized how closely they were standing. Her body was still pressed against his. She could feel the rise and fall of his chest, his breath coming in quick and shallow bursts from the excitement. The sun was beating down on them. She looked up at him and felt his gaze. She felt a swoop in her stomach. Feeling suddenly aware of her bottom lip, she bit it nervously. Was he going to kiss her?

He seemed to read her mind and shook his head before stepping back. "I owe you a drink. After we sign the paperwork tonight, we celebrate," he said. It was more of a statement rather than a question. Stepping to his car, Luc opened the passenger door for her and in climbed a confused and happy Elise.

Chapter Six

After he dropped her off back at the office, Elise got in her car. The drive with Luc had been a blur. Luc had recited facts about the house and regaled her sales tactics as if they were old war buddies. For an instant, she had wondered if she should bring up the night before. But Luc's mind was like a ping-pong ball as he jumped from one idea to the next. Even as she said goodbye, he had moved onto investments that would be made in Shanghai. He drove away in a flash. Elise didn't know what to make of the situation. It had been her easiest and least conventional sale.

Once in her own car, she whipped out her phone and opened the calculator. At six percent of four million, her commission would come in at two-hundred and forty thousand–with only a small fraction going towards Cotherington Realty. She stared at that figure hard until she felt steady enough to drive home.

Back at the condo Rose was laying on the sofa with Langdon on her lap. Elise threw her keys on the countertop and poured herself a glass of water.

"Are you still mad at me?" came Rose's quiet voice from behind the sofa.

Elise took a deep breath. "No–I mean yes–I mean... I don't know," she admitted, rubbing her nose. Elise took a seat next to Rose, whose puffy eyes made clear she had been punishing herself all night.

Tears welled in Rose's eyes. "I'm sorry, again."

Elise put a protective arm around her, feeling too sorry for her to say anything else. "I know you are."

"How am I going to pay them back?" Rose sniffed. Rose wrapped her arms around Elise and cried. Elise grabbed a handful of tissues from the nearby countertop, but Rose's firm grip made it particularly challenging.

With the commission from her sale, Elise could pay off everything as soon as the money was in her account. It wouldn't be ideal, considering that Rose would have learned nothing. Besides, being back at her old house brought back memories. Sure, they had been raised in a wealthy family in a stately home. But their father had still insisted that they get jobs every summer. It was how Elise had met her first boyfriend–scooping ice cream at the golf club.

"I'll make you a deal," Elise began. "What you did was insane. And irresponsible. Wildly irresponsible. But you already know that." Rose nodded, her huge eyes looking heavy with sorrow. "I don't want them coming after you. That's too dangerous. For you, and for me," she said. It was true. She couldn't have some credit union coming after her sister. "We will take care of the loan. But, on one condition..."

The moment she had mentioned taking care of the bank loan, Rose's face crumpled into more tears. "Thank you," was all Elise could hear between the sobs.

Elise wasn't about to go easy on her. "...on one condition," she repeated sternly. "You will go on-line and find a liquidator for that inventory. Even if you have to take ten cents on the dollar, get *something* back. Then we will work out a repayment plan and you will stick to it. I'm expecting a miracle. We can come up with the repayment plan together."

Rose nodded. Elise could tell from Rose's frantic expression that she was trying to come up with a solution on the spot. Still, she wanted to scare her sister a bit. Scare her into working hard and ensuring she *never* got into this kind of trouble again.

"I promise," Rose said. "I promise. I won't let you down."

Later that evening at Cotherington Realty, Elise went to the office and finished the sales documents for Sam. Thinking about that commission, Elise was certain that she was the luckiest girl in the world. She sipped stale coffee at her desk in celebration. Joe meandered over to her and clinked his stained, formerly white coffee mug against hers.

"You've done it again, kid. Couldn't be prouder," Joe said, shaking his head in admiration. "I don't know how you do it."

Elise shrugged. She herself wasn't sure how she had fallen upon such good fortune. Two multi-million-dollar sales within the same month. She wracked her brain for similar instances in the past. She couldn't think of a single instance where this had happened before at the firm. Ever.

"I'm meeting with the client tonight to celebrate. He's thrilled. Who knows, maybe he'll send more business our way?" she told Joe with a smile.

"You go get 'em. And Elise? Don't you fall in love with him and move to France. We need you here," he said with a large guffaw. Elise laughed, but it came out more high-pitched than usual. Don't fall in love, she repeated to herself.

Celebrations that night ensued. Elise wore her new black jumpsuit with taupe open-toe leather sandals. They were comfier than some running shoes she owned. She was meeting Luc at Champain, a swanky bar she had only been to once before on a first-date. With its dim lighting, white marble countertops, and sleek chrome chairs, the atmosphere was young, hip, and about as exciting as it got in Ashfield. It was *the* place to celebrate.

That's how Elise felt as she walked into Champain–celebratory. She had already downed a glass of prosecco before leaving her house to steady her nerves. Only one this time. She didn't know why she felt so nervous, but she chalked it up to the excitement of the sales. This was a turning point for her. Not only career wise, but for her bank account.

Luc was already seated at the bar, an empty chair beside him. He waved her over as soon as their eyes met. As soon as she saw him, she knew she was in trouble. It didn't help that as she got closer she could smell his aftershave.

"Elise," he greeted her, kissing her on each cheek in that way she always saw French people do in movies. Was it her imagination that he lingered on the second kiss?

Smiling, she took a seat and ordered herself a French martini. He drank gin on the rocks.

"So–you're about to be the official owner of the Dalmatian Estate," she told him, flashing a smile. "How does it feel?"

"Wonderful. I'm happy to have that first step over and done with."

Elise's brow furrowed. "First step? Just how many houses are you planning on buying in Ashfield?"

Luc shook his head, a slow grin forming. "Not the first step for Ashfield. First step for you..."

Elise tried to figure out what this meant as he paused dramatically. First step for her? As in them as a couple? Her pulse quickened at the thought.

"... I have an estate in Marseille. Have you ever been?" he said slowly.

Elise shook her head. She wasn't sure if he was asking if she had been to Marseille, France, or his estate. She hadn't been to any of them, so it didn't matter as she shook her head.

"The last time I took a trip was in my final year of university. Then I got a job..." she trailed off. Had it been that long? She winced, thinking about how much she needed a vacation. She resolved she would book one first thing tomorrow.

"It's easy to get caught up in the bustle of everyday life. You miss those, special moments." Luc locked eyes with hers. She was certain this was one of those special moments he had mentioned, as she nodded.

"Yes, so easy." She took another sip at her martini. Feeling bolder, she let Luc in on a little secret. "You know, I grew up in that estate. The one you bought." She paused, waiting for him to look shocked or delighted. But his bemused expression was unsatisfying. "What?" she asked, as he gave her a knowing smile.

"Elise, you think I will spend that kind of money and not do my due diligence and research?"

Elise's mouth dropped open. He had read up on her before? "So, it wasn't the referral from Gerard?"

Luc shook his head with a laugh. "No. That helped quite a lot." He looked serious. "I was looking for someone who understood how I much wanted that house. Someone who would know the ins and outs. Someone who would stop at nothing to get it for me," he said, eyes gleaming.

Elise nodded. "How did you find out my parents had owned that house?"

Luc shrugged. "You can pay to see the sales history of the house. And your last name is uncommon in these parts. I had a hunch you were at least related. Plus, when I mentioned the names of those statues, your face gave it all away," he said, like a detective who had cracked a ten-year-old cold case.

Elise didn't know how to respond. Instead, she took a final sip of her martini and ordered another.

"You know, this is very good news for you. If you want it to be," Luc began. Now he was the one who looked a little nervous. Elise sat up straighter, hanging onto every word. "As I mentioned, I have a place in Marseille. You could say it is, well, similar to the Dalmatian Estate. And I want you to sell it for me."

Elise's drink arrived although she barely noticed. She was too busy studying the lines of Luc's face. The sincerity of his eyes. The dimple on his chin, which she had never noticed before tonight.

"Me?" she echoed.

Luc nodded. "I have already worked with two realtors back in France who could not sell it. Gerard spoke highly of you, and now that I've met you, I want you to be the one to sell it."

Elise nodded, excited for another sale and that Luc wanted her–*her*!–to sell it. First thing first, she snapped into business mode.

"You know, it will take me awhile to gain a license to sell homes in France. A month, maybe longer."

The corner of Luc's mouth twitched. "I can wait."

"Okay, my next question. How much are you thinking of listing it for?"

Luc didn't hesitate for a moment to answer. "Eighty-eight million."

Elise nearly fell off of her stool. She felt dizzy. Surely, she heard that wrong. "Eighty-eight million?" she confirmed. "As in eight-eight million dollars?"

Luc shook his head and relief washed over her for a split second, before he replied. "Euros."

Chapter Seven

Elise didn't sleep a wink. Eighty-eight million euros. Even more when converted into American dollars. The numbers "eighty-eight" kept flashing in her mind like Vegas lights. It was an adrenaline rush just thinking about it. With Luc thrown into the mix, it was enough to make her dizzy.

Marseille. France. Luc had come at her with a slew of facts about the world of luxury French real estate. Marseille, he had told her, was full of contradictions. While the capital of crime in France, it was the capital of culture. The people loved their food. The people loved their cars. Nestled into that realm of fast cars and faster drivers was some of the best seafood in the world. There was also the luxury real estate market. Marseille bordered the French Riviera. Home of the mega-rich, international billionaires, and celebrities–and was a major port city in the South of France. Marseille was *not* the French Riviera, Luc had emphasized. In fact, sometimes people said that Marseille was barely France. Marseille was Marseille. She had to see it to understand. Elise had to admit, it was an enticing sales pitch.

From what she understood, her own sales pitches would have to be enhanced. Competition in Marseille and the French luxury real-estate market was steep. Elise rarely competed in Ashfield's real estate market. She had gotten comfortable. Cushy. When first starting out, she had proved to herself and her team she was more than capable. As Luc had told her right before he left, selling in the South of France had the chance to make her career. It would push her outside of her comfort zone. When was the last time she had felt pushed out of her comfort zone? he had asked.

If she had been bolder, she might have said, "The second he had walked into my life and wanted that estate on Dalmatian Street." She had told him she time to consider the offer. She would sleep on it. But that was a lie, because she did no such thing. Mulling it over in her head, she had talked herself into it and out of it as many times as she had thought about Luc that night.

Which was a lot.

Pros for selling the Marseille mansion: the commission check would be more than her sales combined for the last few years. Getting to spend time in France. Getting closer to Luc.

Cons for selling the Marseille mansion: having to go through the tedious process of gaining a French real estate license. Leaving Rose alone and left to her own devices for the rest of the summer.

It was the latter that made the other pros and cons seem negligible. Whatever good came from selling a multi-million-dollar mansion, she could never justify it if Rose got herself into even more trouble. Rose seemed to need guidance more than ever. Elise was her one and only parental figure. What would happen if she up and left?

When her alarm clock went off at six, Elise was already awake making the first pot of coffee. Sinking into her white leather sofa, Elise took in the views through the floor to ceiling condo windows overlooking Ashfield bay. The sun peaked out from behind the ocean. Langdon sat at her feet and snored. A solitary sailboat was making its way into the harbor. The sky filled with hazy shades of orange, pink, and purple. It was as close to feeling Zen as Elise got–watching those early morning sunrises. With no distractions. Nothing to bother her. No one around.

"Good morning!"

Elise almost spilled her coffee as she jumped in her seat. She whipped her head around. Even Langdon woke from his heavy slumber and stretched. Rose was already dressed and walked at a brisk pace. She had a full backpack she carried in one hand.

"What are you doing up so early?" Elise asked. That startled sensation had nullified any Zen feelings she had been lucky enough to muster. Now she felt annoyed.

Rose sighed. "I am meeting the liquidator at the storage unit. He has a truck arriving in twenty minutes. He told me I will get eight grand in a certified cheque for the inventory. Then I'm starting my new career."

Elise's eyebrow raised. "Career?"

"Yes." Rose didn't elaborate and continued filling her backpack with items from around the condo. A stapler, stacks of printer paper, paper clips...

"Hey, I need those!" Elise said, jumping up and taking two of the four tins of paper clips out of Elise's bag.

"How am I supposed to start a business empire without supplies?" Rose complained.

Elise crossed her arms. "A business empire? Rose, tell me you didn't borrow more money. I thought we talked about this."

Rose shifted from one foot to the other. "Yeah, well, I didn't borrow more money."

"So what's the plan? Aren't you going back to school in three months?"

Rose averted her gaze. "I got an internship. And yes, I'll still be able to go to my classes come September."

Astonished, Elise broke into a grin. "An internship? That's great news! Where?"

Rose bit her lip nervously. "Promise you won't laugh?"

"I promise," she agreed.

Rose shifted before answering. "Leighton-Long Credit Union."

It took Elise a moment to remember where she had heard that name before. When it clicked, she drew an inward breath. "The bank that gave you that insane loan?" she gawked.

"You promised you wouldn't be mad!" Rose shouted, looking wounded.

Elise softened. "Oh, sweets. I'm not mad. I'm just, well, I'm surprised..." she said, doing her best to speak in a gentle tone. "Just to confirm, they are paying you?"

Rose nodded, a glimmer of pride returning. "Above minimum wage too."

"What are you doing there?" Elise prodded.

Rose stared at her feet. "I'm a brand representative intern. I'm shadowing one of the sales guys today. We're heading to a community college about an hour away."

Elise tried to process what her sister was telling her. Her brain felt like a computer short-circuiting. "So, you're selling credit lines to college students? Like that guy did with you?" she confirmed.

Rose glowered. "I know how it sounds. But trust me. I will do things a little differently. Plus, I'll be able to pay you back so fast. They have a fantastic bonus incentive."

Elise winced. This felt like a teachable moment. But before she could say anything, Rose grabbed her things and drank the last of Elise's now lukewarm coffee.

"I've got an appointment I can't miss," Rose said, and blew her a kiss as she walked out of the condominium. The door shut with a heavy thud. Elise knew Rose was putting on a brave face, and that this whole situation had wounded her ego more than she would have ever admitted.

Elise checked the clock which hadn't yet struck seven. She reconciled herself to thinking Rose was maintaining her end of the bargain. Rose had a job. Even if it was at the credit union where she had gotten herself into all that trouble. At least she was showing some responsibility. Or trying to.

Elise knew her parents would have been proud. And for the briefest of moments, she felt a glimmer of hope that maybe, just maybe, she could go to Marseille.

Rhonda Peters was already seated at their usual table at the Ashfield Country Club restaurant. The club overlooked the vast and pristine green landscape. As Elise's best friend since elementary school, Rhonda knew her inside and out. When Elise had first learned of her parents' death, Rhonda had been there within the hour. Rhonda had been the one who heated the casseroles. Rhonda had written up the 'thank you' cards in Elise and Rose's names, in response to the sympathy cards and floral arrangements they had received. Rhonda had counseled Rose and consoled Elise. She had been the one who made her cut back from work and forced her to watch rom-coms instead. It was important to have a balanced life, according to Rhonda. Rhonda was right. She was *always* right.

Over the years, Rhonda had done her degree in psychology while Elise took over the world of real estate. They had grown even closer that past year. Rhonda went through her divorce and Elise struggled to find anyone who could hold her interest longer than a month. As two of the only single women left in their friend-group, they had made biweekly lunch dates at the Ashfield Country Club. It was a wonderful chance for Rhonda to vent, so it wouldn't "spill over to her clients in therapy sessions", as she liked to say. And even though the divorce had been over eight months ago, they had continued the tradition.

"What's going on with you?" Rhonda demanded as Elise arrived late. Elise knew that her sleepless night showed in on her face.

Elise took a seat across from her friend and rubbed her temples. "Rose. Luc. Marseille," she managed. She didn't know where to begin.

Rhonda's eyebrows shot up. "Rose? What's wrong with Rose? You've got it good with that angel."

Even though Rhonda worked with tough young offenders who got sent to her for counseling, Elise knew that Rhonda's assessment was spot on. Rose was, most of the time, an easy sister to look out for. Apart from that awful first year that their parents' had died. Elise exhaled and, after flagging down the waiter and ordering herself a chicken Caesar salad, dove into the details.

"A lot has happened, this has been quite the week," Elise began, before spilling out everything about Rose and the loan. "...and the thing is, it seems like it's come out of nowhere." Rhonda peered at Elise with an unreadable expression. Now it was Elise's turn. "What?" she demanded.

Rhonda exhaled. "That girl has never so much as had a screaming match during that time of the month," she said with a big laugh. "She's in college. She's testing her boundaries. She will screw up here and there. *Let her.*"

As if on cue, Howard Blachner tripped and fell into their table. "Pardon me," he said, fumbling with Rhonda's cutlery. "I'm such a klutz."

Howard was a staple at the Ashfield Gold and Country Club. Divorced with young children himself, after losing his wife following a harrowing year of her undergoing chemotherapy. In the few years since then, he spent his devoted himself to golf.

"It's no problem," Rhonda said, flashing a smile which Howard returned. "Good luck out there today."

"Well, I appreciate your enthusiasm. Hopefully I'm better on the green than I am here on my feet," he said, giving way to another peel of nervous laughter. Elise noticed that Howard's cheeks were pink. Rhonda had sat up straighter. What was going on?

As Howard left, Elise couldn't help but whisper. "Is something going on with you and Howard?"

Rhonda's eyes darted to the tables near them, cautious to ensure no one else heard. "No, yes, I mean, it's complicated," Rhonda admitted, biting down on her bottom lip. "We've been talking. First at the club here, but then he sent me this one email thanking me for the advice I had given him about what fruit to buy in season," she said. "And one thing led to another..."

"Not *sexting*? But... through email?" Elise asked, eyes flashing. She couldn't imagine anyone less likely to sext than Howard. Or Rhonda.

Rhonda shook her head like someone had slapped her. "Elise! Of course not. No. We've been more like pen pals."

Elise bit the inside of her cheeks to keep from smiling too hard. "That is so sweet. How long has that been going on?"

Rhonda fiddled with her cutlery. "A few months. Are you judging me? That's why I didn't tell you because I'm not trying to take the place of Sheila or anything like that. She was such a lovely woman, Sheila. I don't want to sully her memory," Rhonda said, referring to Howard's ex-wife.

"I know that." Elise placed a hand over Rhonda's own shaking one.

Rhonda let out a smile–the kind that made her look ten years younger. "It's so nice having someone to talk to. He's told me all about coping with the loss. I've told him about my divorce."

Elise smiled. "That's great! So why the secretiveness?"

"I don't want anyone to think I'm trying to step in as his wife or as the mother of his children. Three boys," she said, looking stricken.

Elise looked at her friend, knowing her expression was giving it all away. "That's the craziest thing I've ever heard."

Rhonda waived her hands. "Anyway. Enough about me. Tell me, what were you saying about Rose?"

Elise groaned. "But she needs me to help her. I'm a mother-figure to her."

Rhonda barely concealed her laugh. "A better question. Who needs who? Does Rose need you to be a mother, or do you need Rose to stay a little girl? Someone for you to take care of?"

"But I worry about her."

"You always will. Especially considering your history."

"She's got a job at that same bank that she got her loan from," Elise wailed, putting her head in her hands.

"Sounds like she's trying to pay it back," Rhonda countered.

Elise shook her head. "Enough psychobabble. Save it for your clients," she teased. But Elise felt inclined to take Rhonda's advice. Rhonda was the most sought-after child and adolescent psychologist in Ashfield. Elise filled in Rhonda on Luc, the sale, and the even bigger potential sale. She waited with bated breath for Rhonda's response.

"So let me get this straight. That man bought your old house? And he knows it was yours?" Rhonda clarified.

"Well, he didn't know at first. But he took a guess, and I suppose he was right."

Rhonda shook her head. "So is he going to live in it?"

Elise shrugged. "I have no idea. I've never seen him in Ashfield before, but I guess now that he has a home here..." She felt less convinced by her own words the more she spoke. Luc would not be spending tons of time in Ashfield. She knew that. He lived in Marseille. The house had been a test. An expensive test, she noted, but even so.

"And now he wants you to go to Marseille to sell his bajillion dollar mansion?" Rhonda gawked. "Let me guess. He's single, and the two of you will fall head-over-heels like some fantastic rom-com."

Elise laughed. That had been what she was secretly hoping for. But she wasn't going to admit that to Rhonda. Besides, she didn't even know if he was looking for a relationship. She imagined he dated a series of extravagant heiress women with perfect teeth and flawless manicures.

"I blew my chances with him, anyway," Elise said, burying her face in her hands as she winced at the memory.

Rhonda gawked. "You're kidding? But you never date clients." Elise had been asked out before by many of her clients, most of who were recently divorced and looking for a rebound. She always declined, upholding her professional integrity above all else.

"We were celebrating the sale, and I invited him back to my condo. I don't know what came over me." Elise recalled the way she had felt that night. The music. Luc. "Then my heating system broke and the second we walked into my place, it was like walking straight into a sauna." Rhonda laughed as she continued. "I made myself totally available to him. But he didn't make a move. Nothing. He left after fixing my heating system."

Rhonda's laughed faded, and she wiped a tear from her eye and collected herself. "So what? He decided half-way through fixing your heating system he had enough?"

Elise pulled a face. She didn't want to know what Luc thought. "I have no idea. All I know is that he kissed me on the cheek at the end of the night, and we've had this flirty banter back and forth since. I don't know."

Rhonda frowned and made what Elise called her 'psychologist face'. "You know," Rhonda began. "There are a lot of reasons that could have gone down that way. If you continue working with him, you need to clear the air. Get it out in the open."

Elise couldn't have shaken her head fast enough. "No way. I will *not* bring that up. Are you crazy? The night was embarrassing enough. We don't need to talk about it."

Rhonda laughed and held up her hands in mock-defeat. "Okay, okay. So what are you going to do? Are you going to go for it with him?"

Elise shook her head. She wasn't sure if it was out of pride, or her wounded ego. "It's a business relationship," she said in clipped tones. "Besides, I don't even know if I'm going to Marseille yet or not."

Rhonda rolled her eyes. "Is that professional real estate queen Elise talking, or wounded dating Elise?"

Elise wrinkled her nose. "You're right."

Rhonda let out a slow whistle. "Looks like you will send me some nice postcards from the lavender fields."

"But who will watch out for Rose?" she whined, as she rested her forehead in her hands.

"I will, you dope," Rhonda replied.

Elise perked up a bit and took a cautious bite of her chicken Caesar salad. "So you think I should go?"

Rhonda laughed again. "What is with you? Go. Everything will be fine. This is a once in a lifetime chance. Go."

Back at the office, Elise's email was blowing up.

"Way to go..."

"Could I get your advice?"

"I think we would make a great sales team..."

"An interesting offer..."

The news had gotten out about her upcoming sales opportunity in Marseille, which she hadn't even accepted. She had only told one person–Shannon, the new receptionist. She scrolled through her list of emails, which was normally at around ten by the afternoon. Today, she was at sixty. And counting. It was funny how a small amount of success led to old colleagues and acquaintances coming out of the woodwork, just "dying to grab a cup of coffee" with her. She could only laugh.

Researching how to get a real estate license in France was disheartening. It looked much more complicated than she had thought. Even if she wanted to go to Marseille to sell this mansion, getting through all the red tape would delay it all by weeks if not months. She knocked on Joe's door. In all the hubbub, she still hadn't told him about her offer. With all the office gossip, it was about time before he heard it from someone else. That was, if he hadn't already.

"Joe, I need a word..."

"...and I need a word with you, missy!" Joe boomed. Her heart pounded in her chest. He stood up from his plush desk chair and motioned for her to take a seat in the well-worn leather seat across from him. His office was tidy. Elise imagined that at one point, the decor would have been stylish. But now it looked worn and passé. She would have to have a talk with him about hiring an interior decorator to spruce up their corporate image. But that was for another time.

"What would you like to talk to me about?" she asked, crossing and uncrossing her legs. Had he already heard that she had been offered a huge sale with massive commission potential? Did he think she would go rogue and leave the firm? She would never do that. Joe had given her a job straight out of high school, when the other managers at the time had smirked about her being too young, too naïve, too *everything*. But Joe had stood behind her, showing her the ropes of the trade. He had even payed for her real estate examination. It had been on the condition that she stayed with the firm for three years afterwards. It had been over ten years that she had been there, and she had no plans of turning around now.

"Before you say anything..." she began.

But Joe took no notice. "Elise, your sales figures speak for themselves. I want to offer you a partner position here at Cotherington Realty," he said, like he was telling her he had picked her up a cup of hazelnut coffee, which he often did.

Elise opened her mouth but nothing came out. Words escaped her; she couldn't think of a single thing to say. She hadn't expected this. "Partner? But, but I'm not old yet," she blurted out, before clasping her hand to her mouth. "I'm sorry, I mean..."

Joe interrupted her with barrels of laughter. Wiping away an errant tear, he continued. "Yes, I know. That's part of it. I'm looking to slow down. Margaret wants me to spend more time at the golf course with her, less time at the office. And why not? What do I have to prove?" he asked, throwing his hands in the air. "There's no one else I'd trust with this position. You've been here the longest. Trained you myself. Heck, you've trained pretty much everyone else here. We need someone with energy, with enthusiasm, who can... I don't know... bring some style back into this place?" he said, following her gaze to the wilted poinsettia someone had brought in from last Christmas. "What do you say?"

Elise tried to wrap her head around it all. This was happening fast. She had dreamed of becoming a partner, but it was always one day. Now, that day had come. Before she knew it, she blurted out: "Joe, I have to go to Marseille."

"Marseille?" he asked, his eyebrows rising. He clearly hadn't heard the gossip around the office.

"In the South of France. Luc Dubonier, the recent sale I closed on Dalmatian–"

"—your old house, you mean?" Joe asked with a smirk.

Elise pulled a face. Had he known too? "Yes, that one. Anyway, it turns out he liked my sales tactic. He wants me to sell his house in Marseille for, get this, eight-eight million."

"Dollars?"

"Euros."

Joe let out a low whistle and shook his head. "Yowza. Whatever you're doing, kid, keep doing it. You're a money magnet. I'll tell you what," he said, clasping his hands together and taking out a half-empty bottle of whiskey and two highball glasses. "It's a pain trying to get licensed in other countries," he told her, pouring her a generous glass and handing it to her. "But I can set you up with another luxury real estate firm in France. You can work with them? To broker this deal..."

This was music to Elise's ears. She remembered him having brokered some sale in Italy a few years back with another agent. That had been before the agent moved to Italy after falling in love. She couldn't help but laugh. Joe was nothing if not a shameless businessman.

"I would still work under the Cotherington Realty umbrella. Don't you worry," she told him, taking a sip and wincing. Whiskey had never been her drink of choice.

Joe looked lighter. "What do you say? If this Luc guy is serious about selling his house in Marseille, I know the man to partner with. A buddy of mine owns a luxury firm down on the Riviera. It's nice. Margaret and I went a few years back in the fall. Never made it to Marseille though," he said, looking lost in thought. It wasn't before long before he snapped back into action. "Now, you tell this Luc fellow to get in touch. And tell you what–the firm will cover the cost of airfare and the hotel," he added, with an air of finality. "We need you to come back to this firm. My buddy down there can't snatch my best realtor from under my nose," he laughed. "And when you land that sale, you'll come back and join Cotherington Realty as a partner?"

Elise paused for dramatic effect, a warm, tingling feeling spreading all over her body.

"I'm in."

Later that evening at home, Elise sat at her kitchen counter, trying to eat her ravioli without dripping sauce onto her laptop. She pushed her bowl aside, typing 'Marseille' into Google. Images of an old port and even older looking buildings filled her screen. A tingling sensation ran through her whole body. She whipped out her phone and sent Luc a text.

I'm in re: Marseille. Call the Cotherington Realty office for more details.

As she pressed send, a thrill ran through her. It was finally real. The text was poignant, a little mysterious, and aloof. He replied almost immediately–three smiley faces, all upside down.

Elise would have rolled her eyes if she hadn't laughed instead. That was that. She was going to Marseille. She would eat bouillabaisse, drink rose, and walk along the Mediterranean. She could almost feel the sun hitting her face in anticipation.

Earlier, Joe had told her she just needed confirmation from Luc, which from the looks of his text message, seemed like a go. Although it didn't feel real yet, Elise couldn't help but smile. Sometimes, life had a way of shaking things up right when it was least expected. She sent Rose a text message next, asking her to meet for dinner at Frakas. It would be easier to tell her she would be away in Marseille with a big loaf of garlic bread in front of her to soften the blow.

With dinner arranged, a job promotion on the horizon, and an insane commission at her fingertips, Elise felt invincible for only a moment. She had no idea how it was all about to speed up.

Chapter Eight

Elise tore her garlic bread into a million little pieces. The mindfulness meditation she had practiced before walking to Frakas had done nothing to quell her nerves. Then again, the meditation had mentioned nothing about meditating with open eyes. She had sent herself text messages over the course of the ten mindful minutes, adding to her to-do list. Perhaps Rhonda had been right, having once suggested a more proactive approach to relaxation.

"Stop fussing," Mary told her, as she placed a complimentary plate of calamari in front of Elise. "Eat. It'll calm your nerves," Mary said. "You can't tear that apart."

Elise nodded and did as she was told, relishing at how the homemade food had its intended soothing effect. Elise had already confided in Mary all about the deal, the promotion, and Luc. But, all Mary seemed interested in was Luc. This surprised Elise, considering Mary ran her business and was a feminist long before it became mainstream.

"If you could see what I saw–the way he was looking at you," Mary had said, clasping her hands together as if that was that. Now, Elise waited for her sister so she could be able to tell her the good, or not-so-good news, depending whose perspective she took. She expected Rose to be rattled. The two of them had never been apart longer than a long weekend. Often, they traveled together. As kids, they had even gone to the same summer camp. Elise had been a camp counselor when Rose was in the junior cabins. After their parents had died, Elise hadn't even done a long weekend away.

After their parents died, Rose had fallen into a bit of a spiral downward. She began saying things that Elise had never expected to hear from her little sister in a million years. "I don't want to live..." and "I wish it had been me who had died in the car accident..." A psychiatrist, psychologist, and a social worker got involved. Then came the overdose with the medication, followed by a two-month long stint at a youth rehabilitation facility. It was the longest they had ever gone without living together. Still, Elise visited Rose every single day. Even though that was ten years ago, there was still significant fear that came from being separated from her sister. It brought back all those same feelings. After those two-months at the youth rehabilitation facility, Rose emerged stronger and more resolute. Rose became determined to care for her own wellbeing and mental health. Elise had come away from the situation feeling like she had failed her baby sister. How had she allowed Rose to get that bad, right under her nose? That family therapist Elise had met with at the youth rehabilitation facility had ensured her this wasn't her fault. But it hadn't eased those feelings of guilt. Years later, Elise didn't think she would ever shake that worry she felt for her sister.

When Rose arrived at Frakas and took a seat, Elise wanted Rose calm and relaxed before she broke the news.

"How was your day, hon?" Elise asked, placing a protective hand on her sister's arm. Rose examined her with a wary expression.

"Fine," Rose replied, in a way that didn't convince Elise, but she would not press her on it.

"So you'll never guess what house I sold," Elise said, awaiting her sister's response.

"That new condo that went up?" Rose asked, and Elise shook her head.

"Better. And weirder."

Rose rested her chin in her hands, looking bored. "Tell me. You have, like, a million properties for sale all the time. How could I guess?"

"Well, this one wasn't even on the market. Let me give you a clue. It has six-bedrooms, a water fountain with some interesting animals out front..."

Rose's interest piqued. "Not our old house?"

"Yup. This French multimillionaire scooped it up. Weird, huh?"

Rose looked deflated. "Oh. I thought you meant for a moment that you bought it."

Elise's heart sunk. "You know we can't afford that house. If I could, I would. You know that."

"Who bought it?"

"His name is Luc. Luc Dubonier. He's French."

Rose smiled. "Does he deserve the house? Do you think he'll keep the statue?"

Elise nodded. It was still a miracle to her that the current owners had kept it as it was. Somehow, she thought it would be safe. "Well, on a brighter note,

I've got even more news. I'm just going to come out and say it," Elise began. "They have offered me the chance to represent another property. But this one is in Marseille. Luc, that same buyer, has a very lucrative property. I would have to be there for a few weeks. What do you think?" Elise scanned Rose's face for any sign of distress.

Rose took a moment to let it sink in. "Why does he want you to sell it? I mean, why isn't he having some French realtor do it?"

Elise shrugged. She had been asking herself the same question all day. "It's been on the market and many agents have already tried. He liked me. He liked my sales tactics," she explained.

Rose nodded, taking it in. "So you would be gone for a few weeks? I would have the entire condo to myself?"

Elise felt surprised that this was among the first questions on her sister's mind, but didn't let on. "Yes. I mean you'll have Rhonda around if you need anything. She's already agreed to be on call."

"I guess that wouldn't be so bad, me staying at the condo by myself."

"Of course, the terms of the payment plan would remain the same," Elise added, wanting to make sure that her sister didn't think this was a way out of their deal. But it began to sink in that maybe Rhonda was right. Maybe it was her who needed to be a mother figure to Rose, and not the other way around. "And any dates you might have? They can't stay the night," she told her younger sister. Elise realized how silly that sounded, as if she could enforce that rule from overseas. Maybe she could ask Oliver, their doorman, to keep his Irish eyes on the lookout for any unwanted guests.

Rose gave her an angelic smile. "Don't worry. I will take care of everything. That's so exciting about France though! Marseille. I saw an episode on the Food Network about it. Isn't it still, like, dangerous?"

Elise perused the menu but knew that Mary would change her order to the house special anyway. "I guess. I don't know," she admitted. She didn't know about the city at all, apart from what she had seen in pictures and what Luc had told her. "What else do you remember from that episode about Marseille?"

Rose shrugged. "I dunno. It looked pretty. A lot of old buildings. A lot of graffiti. Right on the Mediterranean. They kept focusing on this dish that the city is known for. Bouillabaise."

Elise nodded. She had seen pictures of that signature fish soup.

"All right, my two favorite girls," Mary said, coming over with the two house specials. Tonight it was lamb chops, Greek potatoes, and salad. "*Bon appétit*, I should say," she added with a wink.

Elise and Rose ate in silence, punctuated with a few questions about life in France.

"Oh, and in all the excitement, I forgot to tell you I got offered a partner position at the firm," Elise added between bites of roast lamb. She couldn't believe how she had dropped that into the conversation, as if it was some small detail of her life, and not a mega-huge deal in her career.

"You're kidding. Oh my gosh, Ellie!" Rose jumped up, bypassing the table, and threw her arms around her. "I am so happy for you," Rose said to her, between hugs. If anyone knew how hard Elise had been working that last decade, it was Rose. Elise didn't know if Rose was using her childhood nickname for nostalgia, or to get in her good books before she left for Europe. Either way, hearing it warmed her heart. Rose sat back down and surveyed her with awe. "We've got to order a bottle of champers," Rose declared, before calling out in Mary's direction. "Mary, we're celebrating tonight!"

Elise would have tried to fight her sister if she knew it would do any good. They were celebrating, after all. There was a lot to be grateful for. Mary poured three ample glasses of champagne. Before they left, Mary stopped her and told her she would keep an eye out for Rose. It seemed like the whole town would watch out for her. So now, Elise only had one thing left to worry about.

"Where is that purse?" Elise muttered to herself, as she tossed her belongings into her suitcase. The last two days had passed by in a blur. Elise had barely slept. She made phone calls around the clock. She packed and then made more calls. There was paperwork and more packing. She showed houses to prospective clients. She signed deals and contracts in record time. She wrote all the household instructions for Rose as they came to her. It turned out there was a lot she wanted to tell Rose.

Number 41, she wrote. No strangers in the condo.

Elise wondered if she was being too pushy or paranoid, but she figured it was better to be over prepared than under. Joe had already secured her a hotel in Marseille the day before. "You'd better appreciate this, Elise. This place ain't cheap," he had told her with a grin. But Elise knew for all his whining he was generous. Plus, he could write it all off as part of the firm's expenses come tax season. He had booked her flight. She didn't have time to be nervous, or excited, or anything. She just needed to finish packing.

"Elise, remember that you'll be working alongside Jacques Leveque. He is a French luxury real estate agent," he had told her, careful to pronounce Jacques name slowly and carefully. "Luc Dubonier has already been working with him to sell the estate, with little luck. We're bringing you in as the secret weapon," Joe had told her the day before at the office. "You two will split the commission. We've already got the paperwork drafted." Elise had felt excited upon hearing the news. It felt real, hearing it from her boss. "You will be meeting with him the day after your arrival. His real estate firm is Maison Leveque. A driver will pick you up at the airport," Joe had told her as she jotted down notes. It was a lot of information to gather all at once. It didn't matter if she was ready or not. She had to be.

"I'll miss you," Rose told her as she grabbed a pile of folded clothes at the bottom of her bed and jammed them beside her curling iron and mini-shampoos. Between the two of them, they had fit most her wardrobe into four suitcases. Elise knew she would need another suitcase. There were piles of clothes, shoes, jackets, boots, swimsuits, and a bunch of beach reads. The extra baggage fee was bound to be astronomical.

She would make a crazy commission, feeling a happy glow at the thought. Eighty-eight million. She couldn't even imagine what it must be like to have that much money. She could barely wrap her head around the commission she would be receiving. If she could sell it, that was.

Elise turned to watch as Rose lined up all her suitcases by her bedroom door. Elise took in the way her sister's wavy hair rumpled at the back and the sweet smell of her floral perfume, which Elise had bought for her birthday. Her heart was already breaking and she hadn't even left yet. Rhonda had been right. It was her that needed Rose.

"You be good," Elise said with finality, doing her best to keep her eyes dry, as she sat on her final piece of luggage and Rose zipped it up. She wrapped her sister an affectionate hug. Rose smiled back at her, tears pricking her eyes. Elise took a deep breath, collecting herself. "They're sending a car to bring me there. I'll call you when I land."

Oliver was there when she got out of the elevator to help her with her luggage. "You say you will be gone only for a few weeks, Ms. Laird, but I know how that goes. We'll be missing you around here, that's for sure."

"So I'm wondering if while I'm gone maybe you could..."

"Keep a watch on Rose and report back to you? Consider it done. You haven't changed your cell number, have you?"

The airport limo, if you could even call it a limo, arrived to pick her up and drove her to the Ashfield Airport. Since the driver seemed to avoid the traffic that piled up mid-morning, she over-tipped him. He thanked her as he helped grab her luggage from the trunk–all five bags–and into a cart.

The process as Elise went through the airport was seamless, apart from the exorbitant fees she paid for her baggage. She made a mental note to research how to pack light, going forward. Finally, she relaxed into the uncomfortable plastic chair before boarding. Her phone buzzed. She ignored it at first, thinking it must be work.

I'm on vacation! She thought, before reminding herself this was not a vacation. No, this was work. She had serious work to do. As she checked her phone, a shiver ran through her body as she saw that it was from Luc.

Have a safe flight.

It was a simple enough text. But it filled her with an exhilarating feeling all the same. Elise didn't know if she should text him back or not and instead sent back a smiley face Emoji. Was this how he talked to all his business associates?

The flight itself was unremarkable. Elise popped a valerian and slept through the majority, waking only to eat the complimentary hot meal that went around. Even though she knew that airplane food wasn't good, she couldn't help but enjoy it each flight. Her father, who she continued to consider as the world's biggest food snob, would have been horrified.

The plane landed seven hours later, and she had a short connecting flight over one hour from Paris to Marseille. By the time Elise had landed in Marseille, it was evening back home and close to midnight where she was.

Upon landing in Marseille, a short man with a thick mustache and a deep tan carried a sign with her name printed on it in large lettering. Her own name! Only fancy and important people had those kinds of signs. She walked up to the man, a newfound wave of energy hitting her as she got closer.

"Hi, uh, *bonjour*," she fumbled. "*Je m'appelle* Elise Laird." She did her best to speak her second language despite the feeling of exhaustion that overcame her. She exhaled a sigh of relief that she remembered those words that moment. The driver spoke back to her in rapid-fire French. It sounded nothing like the French she had learned back in school. Her expression must have given away her lack of comprehension.

"English?" he asked her with a smile in a heavy French accent.

She breathed a heavy sigh of relief. "*Oui*, I mean yes. Please."

After collecting all five of her bags, Elise returned to find that the driver had disappeared. What on earth?

"*Ici*!" he called out. Over here!

Elise turned to find her driver wheeling a massive cart, and before she knew it he was tossing her bags haphazardly on top of each other.

"Careful," Elise winced, holding up her hands and pulling a face as her lacquered beige luggage scratched against each other.

"I am Mario," he declared, paying her worries no notice. "I will be your driver while you are in Marseille. If there is anywhere you want to go, you call me." He handed her a business card which besides to working as a driver, showed he was also a local tour guide and artist.

Elise turned the card over in her hand and put it in her purse as they walked to the nearby shiny black town car. Mario pushed the cart.

"And if I want to rent a car myself while I'm here?" She stifled a yawn, not wanting to appear rude, although Mario didn't seem to notice.

Mario shook his head. "*Non madame*. That is not for you. Driver's here, well, I'll let you see for yourself," he said with a laugh. "Unless you too are a fearless driver."

He held open the backseat door to the town car. "Would you mind if I sat up front? I actually get car sick," she told him.

Mario looked surprised and then delighted as he opened up the front door. "M*on plaisir, madame*."

Elise hopped in. "So you're an artist too?" she asked as he sat beside her. Putting the music on to a classical radio station, he began to tell her all about his life as an artist in Marseille. Although it was midnight, he didn't appear the least bit tired. When he spoke, his speech was peppered with French words and pauses. Elise was barely listening, offering *Hmms* and *Ahhs* when it seemed appropriate. She was too busy taking in the early glimpses of Marseille. Mario drove like a seasoned pro, whizzing around parked cars, slow cars, and anyone making a left turn. Other drivers on the road seemed to be playing the same game.

Already, Marseille felt worlds away from Ashfield. It was alive by night. Along the highway leading into downtown Marseille, graffiti-clad warehouses lined the coast. They turned into and proceeded through an underground tunnel, which Mario told her it was the Tunnel de la Joliette, and they emerged onto a busy road and when they arrived at the Old Port. Elise couldn't keep her jaw from dropping. The bright moon glistened over the Mediterranean Sea. All around was the hauntingly beautiful and bustling Old Port. She wanted to be a part of it. She wanted to get out and explore right away.

"Marseille, is it safe?" she asked Mario as the whizzed along the road, remembering Rose's words of caution.

He shrugged. "It's Marseille." As it that explained it all. It wasn't the answer she had hoped for. Marseille certainly wasn't Ashfield.

"...now we are in the Panier district," Mario told her. "Your hotel you are staying at..." he shook his head. "...it is the best in Marseille. And the restaurant? It has a Michelin-star. And it used to be a hospital. The hotel, not the restaurant."

Elise nodded, having recalled Joe telling her as much. As they slowed to a stop, she turned her head. Mario must have made a mistake. Outside of the car, there was only a palace–some sort of historical monument, surely. There didn't seem to be any hotels. A few small restaurants lined the street, lit up from the inside with patrons spilling onto the road.

"Are we stopping?" Elise asked.

Mario turned to her before exiting and opening her door. He gestured towards what she had thought was the historical palace. Now she saw that there was a carpet runner and a doorman.

"*Madame*, welcome to your hotel–La Colombe. In English, it means 'the dove'. *Madame*, welcome to Marseille."

Chapter Nine

After checking into her hotel room—her home for the next few weeks—Elise slept for ten straight hours in her luxurious bed. She was exhausted when they arrived the night before. She barely had taken a moment to assess her surroundings before her head hit the pillow. Waking now, it was noon and golden sunlight poured in from behind the white gauzy curtains. Through the window, a sea of orange terra cotta houses and mountainous green hills rolled in the distance. Something about hotel sheets always made her want to stay in bed forever. Especially when it was a plush, king-sized bed with more pillows than she could count to in French.

Elise checked her phone to see a series of missed calls and text messages. She knew it was no emergency.

Happy birthday!!! Love, Rhonda xox

Happy birthday sis! Call me when you're up!

Joyeux Anniversaire from all of us at Cotherington Realty!

Her penchant to avoid her birthday seemed to fail already. She couldn't help but smile reading her birthday text messages. She had never celebrated her birthday in another country.

This was a big one–thirty. She had the day off before her meeting with Jacques, the owner of Maison Leveque Realty. She had the whole day to herself. As she thought back, she couldn't actually recall the last time she had an entire day with nothing planned. There was no time to lose.

It took only thirty minutes before Elise had showered in the waterfall shower clad with black marble. Black marble appeared everywhere in La Colombe Hotel–from the shower to the elevator to the lobby.

Skipping out of the opulent hotel in an ivory sundress, sunlight dappled against the nearby walls of graffiti. A man wearing a white t-shirt and sunglasses rode by on his bicycle. Maybe I should get one of those? Elise thought, before watching as the cyclist swerved to avoid a speeding car. Perhaps *not*.

Her first stop of the day was the Old Port. Using her iPhone GPS, she navigated her way. More birthday texts poured in from old friends and members of Cotherington Realty. She could get to those later. Her eyes darted into shop windows. She knew she looked like a tourist, but she didn't care. She was in France!

By daylight, Marseille was even more breath taking. She didn't know if she was imagining it or not, but she was certain she could smell croissants wafting out of a nearby patisserie. And was that the sound of the sea?

It seemed almost like a cruel joke that some parts of the world could be so beautiful and others so lacking. As soon as she turned a corner and set foot in the Old Port, she all but let her jaw fall open. The glistening water. The sailboats. The pastel colored buildings lined up side by side in a semi-circle around the harbor. More graffiti. Fishermen yelled to one another good naturedly as they sold their daily catches from wooden booths, with ice chips from their carts spilling onto the gray stone roads. There was a huge, modern and mirrored structure on the water's edge, providing much needed shade as the day was heating up. Marseille felt scrappy, rough around the edges in some ways, and undeniably magical. Marseille felt like a heartbeat of a city. The pulse radiated through her entire body as she strolled through the crowds.

What seemed like millions of boats docked within the harbour. Bustling restaurants with busy patios spilled onto the sidewalks. Elise yearned to know what people were talking about. She listened in carefully, hearing only smatterings of French she couldn't understand. Motorcycles and cars sped past one another on the crowded road. The surrounding buildings were topped with sun-faded terracotta roofs.

In the not too far off distance, a basilica perched above the entire city, as if looking out for every citizen within Marseille. Elise took a bunch of pictures of the scenery on her phone to send to Rose and to post on her Instagram account (#RealtorLife).

"*Excuzez-moi, monsieur*," Elise began, stopping a passerby on the sidewalk. He smiled and frowned, as she tried to put her words together. "*Comment puis je-y aller la*?" she asked, pointing towards the basilica. How can I get up there?

His face softened in comprehension, as he told her the directions. "*La Notre-Dame de la Garde*?" He used hand gestures more as she became more confused.

"*Merci*," she thanked him, as she walked off in the direction he had pointed her, hoping that she had the directions right.

It turns out she had gotten the directions right, but misjudged the height of the hill. To Elise, she was certain she was climbing up a mountain. She was panting by the time she reached the top of the staircase to the Notre-Dame de la Garde, and made a mental note to start exercising the next day.

"...the highest point in Marseille..." she heard British tourists saying as they passed.

Even more magnificent was the giant golden statue watching out over the city at the very top. Elise lit candles for her parents. She said a few words of silent prayer before leaving.

Elise had heard that Marseille was a dangerous city, but she found everyone she met to be respectful and kind. Of course, she stayed in the well-traveled, touristy downtown region. She knew there was another side of the city she would never see.

Snapping back to the present moment, a tourist passed by Elise. Something distinct caught Elise's eye. A spherical gold handbag with gold and pearl chain. It flashed through her mind that the same one her mother had always carried with her. As far as she knew, purses by L'Or and D'Or were nearly impossible to find in the States.

Memories of her mother with that handbag hit her like a ton of bricks. Elise had often starred at that handbag, which she mother had brought with her *everywhere*.

"*Excusez-moi*!" Elise called to the woman, before she could help herself. Luckily, the woman was part of a British tour group. Elise jotted down the name of the store where she had bought it. *Yesterday*. She felt like skipping for joy as she thanked the girl. It was her birthday, after all. And she had never owned a L'Or and D'Or bag before.

A 'grownup handbag', as she had always thought of them, was something she had wanted since she was a little girl. Up until this point, Elise had relied on the same makeshift nondescript beige bag for years. A jolt of excitement hit her as she typed in the name of the store in her GPS, and the descent down from the basilica felt speedy by comparison. Her focus fixed on L'Or and D'Or with each step.

L'Or and D'Or was *expensive*. In addition to the brand scarcity in the States, it was another reason why Elise hadn't bought one herself. It had been a gift to her mother from her father on their honeymoon (coincidentally in France). Her mother had always carried it, and Elise was too precious about her mother's heirloom piece to use it. Now, she wanted one of her own. One to take with her *everywhere*. It had been her mother's signature. Besides, Elise had always secretly coveted handbags. Since she was young, she had known all the staples. The Birkin. Lady Dior. Vuitton's Speedy. Now, it was her turn.

The L'Or and D'Or shop was more than she could have imagined. Visions of her mother and father there—or at least another store in France—came to her imagination. Retracing what she believed to be their steps, Elise found what she was looking for. Elise chose a soft gold spherical handbag with tiny pearl accents, the elegant interlocking L and D in gold script. With a ruffle of tissue, Elise beamed as she left the store, taking the purse out of the bag immediately. It felt like one with her as it swung from her shoulder. This L'Or and D'Or purse would be her new 'signature'. With a fancy L'Or and D'Or handbag, wasn't she practically French now anyway?

She was feeling like birthdays might be worth celebrating.

It wasn't until the late afternoon that she was crossing the street with some extra shopping bags that the blast a car horn stopped her in her tracks. Elise leaped backwards, her heart racing. A red convertible was stopped, the driver glaring at her. Forget herself—she clutched her handbag which narrowly escaped the hit. She breathed a sigh of relief as her heart thudded in her chest.

The driver, a man with bleached hair, began yelling at her incomprehensibly in French. Elise pulled a face. There was no way she was fluent enough to understand French when it was coming at her that fast, and that angrily. Perhaps this was the Marseille that she had read about.

"*Je m'escuse*," she called out, holding her hands up as if to signal her defeat. She didn't want any trouble. She had been in such a daze taking in the city, sights, and smells. She hadn't realized the pedestrian light had turned red.

The driver shook his head, muttered something under his breath, before his eyes darted to her purse. "*Mais joli sac*," he said to her and drove off. Nice purse. She clutched it to her side, all the while admiring the way it felt hanging off of her shoulder. *This* was why you got a nice handbag, she thought. It was appreciated by one and all. All the way back to La Colombe Hotel, Elise couldn't help but laugh at the ridiculous tattoo the man in that car had sported. Stars across his chest, which were visible thanks to the low-cut V-neck t-shirt he wore.

The doorman held open her door with a nod of his head and Elise smiled in return. Feeling flushed from her escapades, she walked though the black-and-white marble lobby, the afternoon light pouring through the skylight above, when the concierge flagged her down.

"*Madame* Laird? You have a visitor," the concierge said. Elise had to look no further than the seated reception, where she saw Luc sitting on a minimalist beige sofa. Her heart sunk into her stomach and turned to butterflies. What was he doing here?

"Welcome to Marseille," Luc said as he walked over, greeting her with a kiss on each cheek. It would take her a while to get used to that custom, she thought, as she suppressed the urge to give him a big hug.

She beamed back at him in response, taking in his bright expression. "It's good to be here," she said, and she meant it. Their eyes locked and her legs felt like they were about to melt beneath her right there in that lobby. She looked away and pushed an errand stand of hair behind her ear.

He stepped back a moment to survey her. "You look good here," he declared.

Elise felt herself flush and laughed. It came out more high pitched than she had intended. "Where? In this lobby? In Marseille?"

He shook his head. "Both, I suppose." Elise smiled and jutted out her hip with a playful wink. She couldn't believe the confidence that had washed over her. She felt good. "Well, I suppose I wanted to come over and see that you arrived all right. You know, Marseille isn't the safest city. So I wanted to make sure you were, you know, all right."

Elise's heart thudded in her chest. Before she could reply, the concierge came over again. "And *Madame* Laird, would you like your birthday champagne sent up now or later?"

Elise's eyes widened. Birthday champagne? She opened her mouth to reply, before realizing this must be a gift from Joe and the team at Cotherington Realty. They were the only ones apart from Rose who knew where she was staying and her birthday.

"Later is fine," she said, trying to brush it aside. "*Merci*."

Luc's eyes widened. "Ah, it is your birthday?"

Elise nodded, averting her gaze to a modern art piece nearby. She hated celebrating her birthday. Today had been perfect. Low-key, some shopping, *the end*.

But Luc continued. "Well, we must celebrate. You have plans tonight, or non?"

"No, but—"

"Ah, ah, ah," Luc held up his hands, as if to signal he had won. "I won't take no for an answer. Luckily, you are staying at my favorite hotel in Marseille, which has one of the best restaurants. Three Michelin-stars, too," he added with a wink.

Elise flushed. Okay, so her arm wouldn't need to be twisted too much to go out for a dinner with Luc Dubonier. Especially when the words 'Michelin' and 'star' were included. "Okay," she finally agreed with a smile. She and Rose had wanted to go to a three-star Michelin restaurant since, well, *forever*.

As Luc reserved a table for them later that evening, Elise's entire body tingled. Was this it? A do-over to their disastrous-ending first and only date? If it had even been a date. She was still unclear where they stood with one another.

When Luc turned to her and announced he had made them reservations for seven o'clock that evening, his face was telling. "I'll see you tonight," he added with another wink. Elise smiled. Suddenly her birthday seemed like the best day in the world.

Chapter Ten

Talking on the phone with Rose occupied most Elise's evening, as she got ready for dinner. As Rose coached her on the best way to apply liquid liner, Elise calmed her nerves with a glass of wine.

"So you're going out with Luc tonight?" Rose asked her over the phone.

"*Mhm*," Elise replied, in what she thought was a nonchalant tone.

"You know," Rose pressed. "You've barely said two words about him to me. Like, literally nothing. What's going on with you two? He flies you out to Marseille –"

Elise jumped in. "He's not paying for my flight out here. Cotherington Realty is paying, because I'm going to bring home a big fat commission check," she explained. She had laid out all the terms and agreements with Joe before she left and they were still fresh in her mind. She picked up some highlighter and began applying it to the tip of her nose, like Rose had taught her. An "instant nose job" effect, Rose had told her, which Elise hadn't known at the time whether to be grateful or offended by.

"Anyway even so, he wants to spend time with you," Rose countered.

"Maybe," Elise said absently. She had avoided telling Rose about her mishap inviting him to her condo. But that bumpiness seemed to have been smoothed over anyway. "But I'm also a fantastic real estate agent. Hey, have you been seeing anyone?" Elise asked, trying to change the subject.

"No, ever since Kelsey and I broke up, it's been slim pickings. There's literally no one new in this town," Rose told her. Elise did know. The Ashfield dating pool was miniscule. It would be hard to find someone new to date whose friend, cousin, or sibling you hadn't already gone out with.

"Ah, well. Better luck next time. I'm going to say goodbye now," Elise said, as she eyed the slinky gray dress she had brought with her in case of a special occasion. She suddenly wished she had brought a second pair of Spanx.

"Are you pushing me off?" Rose asked in mock offence.

"Yes, and only 'cause I love you. I need to slither into this dress now."

"The gray one?" Rose asked with a teasing tone. "You're going to have to do more than slither," she said laughing.

"Rude!" Elise responded. But it was true. It was more likely that she was going to need to squeeze herself into it, and risk tearing the dress.

"You're sooo into him," Rose laughed. "Happy birthday and text me how it goes!"

Elise said a final goodbye and hung up. After shimmying herself into the skin-tight dress, which took three tries, she examined herself in the mirror with a scrupulous eye. The dress gave her cleavage she never had. And the Spanx was working a minor miracle. She had to admit—she looked good. It wasn't a bad way to start a new decade, she reluctantly admitted to herself, before traipsing out to celebrate with her new L'Or and D'Or purse flung over her shoulder.

Luc met her downstairs at in the lobby and gave her an appreciative once over as she stepped out of the elevator.

"Don't you look *magnifique*," he said, holding up an elbow for her to hold as they walked into the restaurant. As the waiter led them to their table, a hushed silence fell in the room as the other patrons saw Luc.

"People here know you or something?" she hissed in his direction, as a couple looked up from their wine.

Luc laughed and whispered into her ear. "I think they're all looking at how beautiful you look tonight."

Elise felt herself turn pink from her neck all the way to the tips of her ears.

They took their seats alfresco, overlooking the Old Port of Marseille and a direct view of the Notre-Dame de la Garde. Elise felt like she had known Luc for years. The lights of the city glimmered below, the fading sunlight leaving the sky a golden haze. At that moment, it seemed silly not to celebrate a birthday. Elise didn't know why she hadn't enjoyed celebrating in the past. She wished *every* day was her birthday.

"So," Luc began, as their wine arrived. A Châteauneuf-du-Pape. "You know all about me and where I went to school, my first jobs, all of that," he said, waving his hand. "I know nothing about you."

Elise cocked her eyebrow. "What do you want to know?" she asked cautiously, placing her napkin in her nap.

"Oh, everything, you know. Just your most private details and secrets," he fired back with a grin.

She laughed. "Okay, well. I grew up in Ashfield, but you already knew that," she said, referring to his earlier research into her. "I grew up on Dalmatian Street in that–your–house." After all this time, she still found it strange that other people owned that house. "But it's just Rose and I now."

Luc's eyebrows shot up. "Oh?"

To her own surprise, she allowed herself to open up. "My parents were in a car accident," Elise told him, taking a slow sip of wine. She allowed herself to lapse into memory about that day. "Ten years ago. To nearly the day. It's still a hard time for me," she admitted. She hadn't celebrated her birthday since.

Luc nodded. "I understand. It's just you two, then?"

Elise nodded. "Yeah. Me and Rose. She's a sweetheart. She's in college now, but still trying to figure out what she wants to do."

"Aren't we all?" Luc laughed. He ordered for them in perfect French–seared scallops, oysters, bouillabaisse, and squid and artichokes. It was a seafood-heavy menu, which Elise was grateful for.

"You do like fish?" Luc asked, looking horrified he hadn't checked sooner.

"Love. Love *love* fish," she said with enthusiasm. "My dad actually got his start as a fisherman on the boats, before he became a restaurateur. He loved fresh oysters," she divulged. She didn't know why it was all coming out–all of this information about her parents. She hadn't talked about them in years. She chalked it up to nerves, jet lag, and the wine.

"He sounds like he was my kind of man," Luc said. "You must know about bouillabaisse then?"

Elise shook her head. "It's not something we have much of in Ashfield."

Luc perked up. "Well, it's a staple of Marseille. At least, it used to be," he added in a rueful tone. "In recent years, the prices of it have soared. It is no longer a fisherman's dish for the everyday working man or woman. Now, you can find it for eighty euros, sometimes more, at restaurants. Some is fantastic, some of it is..." he pulled a face. "... for tourists, I suppose."

Elise pulled a face. "That's a shame."

"The base," Luc began, his face lighting up. "The holy trinity. Saffron, fennel, and oranges. Since Marseille has always been a melting pot of a city..."

"... what do you mean, melting pot?" Elise interrupted.

"I mean, it's always been a city of immigrants. Where people come with what they have. And since Marseille is a port city, we had exotic ingredients brought in that are now part of the staple cuisine. Hence, saffron, fennel, and oranges being the staples of bouillabaisse. The fish that the fishermen used to make bouillabaisse are some of the ugliest fish you'll ever see," he said, breaking into a laugh.

Elise couldn't help but smile. "Really?"

"Oh yes. They are practically unsellable at fish markets. Just hideous," he said with disdain, pulling a face and making Elise laugh. "So they used them as the fish in bouillabaisse. No one wanted them. Now, everyone wants it. At a high price too."

After they ordered a second bottle of wine, a cote-de-provence rose, at Elise's insistence. "I can't come to provence and not have the rose," she told him. "It's kind of a thing in America. Rose all day."

Luc scrunched his eyebrows together. "What kind of thing? Like, a social media thing?"

"Exactly. On every girl's Instagram account during the summer, you'll find that as the tagline," she explained.

Luc shook his head. "That I will never understand. I like to keep my dealings private."

Her eyebrows shot up. "But for such a successful family, is that even possible?" Elise began as the waiter arrived with a massive silver platter, filled with ice and oysters. The waiter explained the origin of each type of oyster and the tasting notes.

As Elise slurped one oyster, she closed her eyes in delight. "I've never had someone explain to me the tasting notes of an oyster before."

Luc laughed. "You have never been to France then," he said, clinking his glass to hers. Elise took a sip of the rose—dry, floral, aromatic. While her father had been the restaurateur and foodie, it had been her mother who had taught her how to discern the notes in wine.

"I love it here," Elise proclaimed, as she took it all in. The crisp white tablecloth. Melodic music played in the background. The view. Sure, she had already drunk a half bottle of wine. But she meant it.

"The restaurant or Marseille?" he asked, looking amused.

Elise shrugged. "Both, I suppose. I love how vibrant and alive Marseille feels. And this restaurant, well, I don't even know if *parfait* describes it."

Luc's eyes lit up. "That is what I love about Marseille too," he began. "I mean, anyone can feel at home in Marseille. After the plague hit Marseille way back when, the city was decimated. Two out of every three people died. The rest of Provence isolated us, even creating a plague wall. But due to waves and waves of immigration, our population recovered in only forty years. It's taken other cities nearly twice as long, some even longer than that... but what I love about this city is that anyone can walk into Marseille and make it home. They can come home."

Elise nodded, taking his words into consideration. "You really like your history, don't you?"

Luc's eyes shone. "Who doesn't?"

"I like your take on what makes Marseille an amazing city, too. I agree. It's all of what diversity, what makes the city a melting pot, that makes it so alive and vibrant."

Luc peered at her and took another sip of wine. "How old are you turning today, if I might ask?" Then he held up his hands, shaking his head. "I'm sorry. That is so rude of me."

Elise paused for a moment and shrugged. She was sure there were many women who would have fudged the numbers or have taken offence. But today, she couldn't care less. "Thirty," she said brightly.

He laughed. "That is an easy one or a tough one. Which is it for you?"

Elise took a moment to consider the question. Sure, it had been a successful past couple of years. She had succeeded at work. She was about to become the youngest partner at the realty firm. She owned her own condo. Albeit, with a mortgage that she was trying to pay off as fast as she could. "I am really happy with my success," she said, choosing her words carefully.

"A diplomatic answer," Luc nodded. "But do you have what you want in life? Outside of work, I mean."

Elise didn't know what to say. This was like when a teacher put her on the spot in math class. She had never known the right answer.

Luckily, Luc jumped in, saving her from his own question. "Because I'm only a few years older than you, and I still feel like I don't know." He downed the remnants of his rose. His candor surprised her.

Elise paused, deciding to open up too. "I suppose," she began, twisting her fingers around her wine glass. "I wish I had fallen in love by now," she said, scanning his face for any sign that she had said the wrong thing. She wasn't sure if it was the wine or the company. "I mean, sometimes it would be nice to have a partner to help pick up the slack. Someone to, you know, share it all with."

Luc looked at her in a stunned silence, making Elise wish she had said nothing at all. "You have never been in love?" Luc asked.

Elise shook her head and surprised even herself by laughing. This was by far the worst thing she had ever divulged to a man she hardly knew, but for some reason the words kept spilling out. "I've never had a relationship more than a month," she admitted. "Unless you count, like, my college boyfriend."

Luc bobbed his head from side to side, considering this. "Well, I suppose you would count him, if it was serious?"

Elise felt transported to memories of her and Jackson–attached at the hip, everyone thought they would be the first to get married. But, after her parents' car crash, everything seemed to unravel. She threw herself into her schooling. When she wasn't studying, she was trying to spend as much time with Rose as she could. Then there was the matter of settling the estate. Suddenly, the thought of having a boyfriend had felt trivial. As she told this to Luc, he looked heart broken on her behalf.

"Yeah, I suppose it was a relationship," she admitted. "But not anytime recently."

Luc nodded like he understood, and Elise wondered what his story was. She observed as he took a thoughtful sip of wine, just as their main courses arrived. Their conversation steered towards less touchy subjects–good food, travel, the real estate market. He seemed fascinated by her interests as she was, much to her delight. By the time she was finishing the last few bites on her plate, she wished she could do it all over again.

The sun set over Marseille, filling the sky with hazy pink and orange clouds. Elise broke the silence that had fallen over the table as they ate. "So you never spilled about your past relationships," Elise blurted out. The waiter poured the last of their wine into their glasses.

Luc laughed as he squirmed in his seat. Now that the spotlight was on him, did he feel uncomfortable? Elise would have changed the subject if it were anything less enthralling. She wanted to know.

"Things are, complicated in my life," he said warily. "And I've been meaning to apologize," he said, looking at her. "About my behavior at your home."

Elise felt shocked beyond words. She hadn't expected that. "Oh, it's all right," she fumbled, unsure of the correct way to respond.

He shook his head, as if annoyed with himself. "Again, I don't want to get into it. But, well, things are complicated. I don't want to drag you into anything. I didn't want to drag you into anything..." He looked at her, searching for face for a sign that she understood.

What did that mean? Was he getting a divorce? What was the deal with his ex? Instead of asking questions, Elise nodded. "That's okay. Thank you for saying that though, anyway."

"Thank you. Your hard work, your devotion to what you do, your energy. Thank you for coming all this way. Having you here makes me thrilled," he said, running his hand through his hair.

She realized he had skilfully evaded her question about past relationships. She wouldn't press him on it. For someone so open about so much of his life, he was surprisingly secret about other things.

For now, it gave her a thrill to hear him say having her there made him happy. The waiter arrived with their bill, and Elise offered to pay for her half. He waved her card away.

"Nonsense. It has been my pleasure to dine with you this evening," he said. "And besides, no one should have to pay for dinner on their birthday," he added with a wink. Elise felt herself blushing. This whole birthday thing was looking up.

As she stood up on her feet, she realized that she might have miscalculated just how much wine she had drunk. She grabbed the table to steady herself.

They left behind the sparkling chandeliers and the stunning views of the restaurant. Back in the lobby of the hotel, Elise didn't have to go far to get back to her room. It flashed through her mind to invite him up, but she thought better of it. They still had a long road of working together. She didn't want anything to get awkward.

Thanking him for the birthday dinner with an oh-so-French kiss on each cheek, she seemed to go in the same direction as him–their faces narrowly missing the other.

"Sorry," she laughed, feeling self-conscious. So much for not wanting things to get awkward.

"*Bon nuit*, Elise," Luc said, as he gave her shoulders a gentle squeeze. "I will see you tomorrow. At my house."

Unlike a date, where the prospects of seeing the other in the future was always up in the air, Elise had concrete and firm plans to meet with the mogul. Tomorrow. She gave him a quick wave, her heart feeling like it would explode from happiness, and pressed the button to the elevator. Once Luc was out of her sight, she allowed herself to grin like an idiot.

"*Bon nuit*?" the elevator attendant asked her, after it arrived. Good night?

Elise nodded, doing her best to contain her smile. "*Oui*," she replied. "The best."

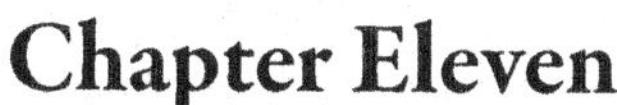

Chapter Eleven

The following morning, Elise awoke bright and early. She was meet Jacques Leveque, the owner of Maison Leveque, who she would work alongside throughout the sale of Luc's house. It was an unconventional arrangement, but Joe had lobbied on her behalf. Jacques had eventually agreed. It was the fastest way to allow for Elise to work on the sale of the house without having to get a French real estate license. She would show the house and Jacques would take care of the rest.

At least, that's how Joe had laid it out to her.

Besides, Jacques had had no luck finding a buyer for the property anyway. The least they could do was try another listing agent and split the commission. On a house of that caliber, it would be a record-breaking commission either way.

She was scheduled to meet Jacques for breakfast at La Bernadette, a restaurant in the Old Port, where she planned to get herself a cafe crème and a croissant. She didn't care if it was cliché.

In her most professional outfit she had brought with her–a navy fitted blazer, white stiff-cotton knee length dress with little pleats around the waist, and navy kitten heels–she set off to conquer the world. Or at least, that's what she told herself. The phrase "Conquering the world" had a comforting and focussing sound and was a saying passed down from her dad that both she and Rose often used. Of course, today her new L'Or and D'Or handbag accessorized it.

It only took seven minutes of walking along the streets of Marseille before her kitten heel had gotten stuck between cobbled stones on a stairwell. Her foot came out of her shoe as she caught herself against the handrail with one hand while protecting the handbag with the other. She did a quick inventory to see if she had hurt herself but everything seemed to be intact. So far, so good but she had a feeling that that had been a sign that today of all days, she needed to pay attention to detail. She passed ancient buildings, graffiti, and Marseillais taking their motorcycles to work. The smell of diesel fumes from the cars reminded her of her dad's old cars he used to work on in his spare time. Using her phone as a GPS, she arrived at the cafe early.

Taking a seat overlooking the harbour, the gentle breeze made sitting in the bright morning sun feel bearable. The humidity in the air suggested a scorching hot day ahead. She sent Jacques a quick email him what she was wearing and where she was sitting. She hadn't been there for long before a red convertible whipped by. It came to an abrupt stop and parked in front of the cafe. A man with bleached blond hair, sunglasses, and startlingly white teeth stepped out.

Elise did a double take. Then it hit her. The bleached hair. A star tattoo peaking out of his button-up shirt became visible. He had left the top couple buttons undone. As he stepped out of the car, he didn't seem to take any notice of her. He strode out of his convertible and onto the same cafe patio as her, taking a seat at a nearby table facing the water as he checked his phone. Out of the corner of her eye, she caught him glimpse in her direction. As she turned to face him, he wasn't looking at her–or he was looking at her bag. Doing a double-take himself, he averted his gaze back to his phone.

She glanced over again, and he now looked from his phone to her. With an air of displeasure, he stood up and walked over.

"Elise?" he asked in a heavy French accent.

"Jacques?" she asked cautiously. Surely this wasn't him. It couldn't be.

But he nodded, clearly looking uncomfortable as she was. He appraised her from head to toe and seemed to make a split decision that she would have to do.

"Very nice handbag," Jacques said finally with a gleam in his eye, before taking a seat at her table across from her. He flagged down a waiter and ordered himself a croissant and cafe crème. Elise did the same.

"A bag like that should have a name," Jacques continued, taking out a cigarette and lighting it. He blew a plume of smoke towards the port. Elise had met men like him before. She needed to beat him at his game.

"How about Lord? 'Lor' for L"Or and 'D' for D'Or," Elise suggested with a playful grin.

"Lord," he nodded, the corners of his mouth moving up a millimeter. "I like it."

"Nice running into you again. Although this time, on safer ground," she grinned. Sometimes, the easiest way out of a tricky social situation was to address the elephant in the room right away. It had also backfired on her before. She kept her fingers crossed.

"Yes," Jcaques agreed coolly. "Now, Luc Dubonier. Luc Dubonier. What a property, no?" His eyes lit up like a child on Christmas morning. If there was one thing this man cared about, she could tell, it was luxury. From his take on her purse to his expression while talking about Luc's property.

Elise smiled. "I have yet to see it. But from what I hear–"

"—It is simply fantastique," Jacques interrupted. "Unparalleled. You know Le Pharo?" He peered at her from behind his sunglasses, as if to say that she *should* know Le Pharo.

Luckily, she did.

Elise nodded, knowing only the iconic ancient mansion in the heart of Marseille from her Google searches. Jacques barely concealed his relief to be working with someone who at least knew that much.

"Le Pharo is beautiful. I plan on visiting it tomorrow," she told him.

"Well, Luc's property is even better than that. *C'est fantastique*."

She felt him warming to her as he winked in her direction as their cafe crèmes arrived. Jacques and Elise spent the next hour pouring over details. Comparing notes. Comparing past sales. As the owner of Maison Leveque, one of the most successful realty firms in the South of France, his sales record gave Elise a run for her money. He showed her a picture of yet another seaside mansion he had sold.

"And this one here, it has not two, but three swimming pools," he told her. Elise's eyes were wide. She hadn't ever seen such a myriad of luxury homes before, all within such a small radius. In Ashfield, there were nice homes. Stunning homes. Homes that were often featured in magazines, showcasing picture-perfect small town life. But nothing like this.

"The *good* celebrities live on the Riviera," he boasted. "Elton, Bono..." Jacques listed off a few more names. Elise shook her head in awe. She wondered if he had sold any of their houses, but something told her that while he may be showy, he was discreet. There was a reason Luc had chosen to work with him.

"And do you sell a lot of homes in Marseille then?" she asked him.

Jacques shrugged. "I sell a lot of houses everywhere."

"So, how did Joe know to get in touch with you?" she asked him.

Jacques responded breezily. "Joe and I met traveling back when we were both in our twenties. We kept in touch through the years. I actually visited Ashfield recently," he explained. Elise was surprised. Jacques seemed so much younger than Joe. But then again, that was the beauty of the cosmetics industry these days. A few of her friends had Botox and fillers done regularly. She had only gone once herself–her phobia of needles keeping her from making it a habit. She looked a little more carefully at Jacques' face to see if there were any tell-tale signs of Botox. Either he was a dermatologists dream, or had very expert work done.

"So you're alright with this arrangement?" Elise clarified. She wanted to make sure that they were on the same team. From experience, she had learned that sales went the best when the entire team was on board.

Jacques shrugged before taking another drag of his cigarette. "If you can get us a sale at the listed price, then I'll say it has been worth it."

Elise nodded. "That's the goal."

"Plus," Jacques continued. "I have been trying to get this sale for ages. It's tough," he relented. "There aren't that many people with that much liquidity. We're looking not for a millionaire, but a billionaire," he explained.

Elise nodded. "And are there many of those in these parts?"

Jacques smiled. "*Mais oui.* You have to know where to look. I haven't seemed to be in the right place at the right time."

The two of them finished their second round of cafe crèmes. The sun was rising higher in the sky and Jacques had already asked the waiter to put up their table umbrella.

"Much better," he said, fanning himself. "How do you know Luc anyway?" he asked, lighting another cigarette.

"I sold him a house in Ashfield."

Jacques nodded. "Nice town, Ashfield. I'm guessing you know all the details about why he's selling this place then."

Elise shook her head. It hadn't occurred to her he might sell for any reason. In fact, she hadn't thought of that at all. Whenever she had thought of his house, the only thing that came to her mind was eighty-eight million euros.

"No, I don't," she admitted.

Jacques eyes widened. "You're joking?" he said in delight. "Well, I'll tell you everything..."

Any ice that had laid on the surface when she had first met Jacques soon thawed, as he recounted to tell her the details of Luc's life. He told her about how Luc's mother died when he was born, and he had a successive string of stepmothers. "Some good, some not-so-good..." he explained. His most recent stepmother had lasted a good test of time. She had been with their family since Luc was ten years old. "Now, that is just over twenty years," Jacques explained. Then, Luc fell in love with Karina Karrentin, a girl he had gone to school with. "Luc finally asked her to marry him. And they had the most elaborate engagement party ever. I mean, seriously. Press were camped out outside of their estate. It was *extraordinaire*." Jacques told her. "Right after the engagement party, they called off their engagement. Two-months after that, his dad died," he said sharply.

Elise felt like her brain was short-circuiting. Had she heard that correctly? Luc Hadn't mentioned anything about that at dinner.

"That's terrible." Elise said eventually, frowning.

Jacques nodded. "Luc couldn't handle it, or at least that was the rumor around town. He ended up leaving–traveling for months on end. No one knew where he was. The Dubonier Entreprise, which his father had run up until then, was suddenly the responsibility of Luc. But..." Jacques paused. "...Luc didn't seem to care. The rumor mill is unreliable. But some people said he was trying to win back Karina, some said he was doing some kind of pilgrimage to honor his father. I mean, their family is famous around these parts. You say the name 'Dubonier' and people turn their head. That family is money."

"How did they make it all?" Elise asked. She was happy Jacques was so free flowing with this kind of information. She would never have been able to ask Luc. No wonder he had been evasive when she had asked about his love life earlier.

"Newspapers," Jacques said pointedly. The grandfather started it all. And now they own all the radio stations and news programs across the country. In most of Europe. I heard they were looking to even expand into the United States."

Elise nodded, remembering that she had also heard that from Joe.

Jacques continued. "And Luc is private too. Pri-vate. He does not like his dirty laundry aired for the entire world to read about. That whole family was pretty hush-hush. You know? Apart from that big, fancy engagement party." He took another drag of his cigarette.

Elise nodded. "But I Googled his name. Nothing about any of this came up."

Jacques scoffed. "Paid off every newspaper and reporter in France they didn't already own, I expect. Anyhow. That poor man has been through the works this past year. The least we can do is get him a good sale." He extinguished his cigarette in the ashtray before lighting up another. Elise's eyes watered from the smoke. The no-smoking campaigns that had been implemented back when she was in school had done their job. She had never had so much as a puff, believing that her lungs would instantaneously metastasize into cancerous masses.

Jacques continued talking about the dramas, the highs and the lows of the elite within the South of France. He seemed to know everything about the goings-on of that world. So much for discreet. Elise couldn't help but dwell on the fact that the night before, she had told Luc everything about her own losses. Her parents. How hard it had been.

He hadn't said a word.

To his credit, his loss was much more recent. It was challenging to wrap her head around. She couldn't imagine how he felt–getting dumped by his fiancé and losing his father in such a brief window of time.

"Why does Luc trust you anyhow?" Jacques asked out of the blue, his eyebrows raised in her direction. This man had no filter and didn't seem the least bit concerned about offending her.

"Why does he trust you?" she countered.

Jacques fired back. "I have the most successful sales records of any realtor in the South of France. While I might not have the fastest sales, I sell big and I sell high." Elise couldn't help but stifle a giggle at how seriously he took himself. "Now, you go."

"Truthfully," Elise began. "I'm good at my job. I got him a house that wasn't on the market in Ashfield."

Jacques eyebrows raised even further. "That's it?" he asked, a telling look on his face. Elise exhaled in frustration. Sure, she had almost had a fling with Luc.

But now their relationship was strictly business. She didn't have to prove herself, she reminded herself, not to Jacques.

"Yes," she said, mustering as much dignity as she had. "That's it."

With his sparring partner out, Jacques backed off. "Okay. I was just asking. You seem like a nice woman. Luc could use someone nice, for a change," he said with a shrug.

Elise wanted to ask him more about what he meant by that, but before she could get a word out, Jacques continued. "So–you ready to take a look at the famous Marseille mansion? I will take notes for you. Just in case you miss something," he said. It was evident that he was not convinced that she was up for the challenge of selling the property. "It's pretty easy to get swept up in the grandeur of it all."

Elise scoffed. He didn't need to take that condescending tone with her. She was a professional. She would be fine handling it. But she said a polite *merci* all the same.

Jacques stood up and thanked the waiter. "Ready?" he asked.

Elise took a deep breath. "I'm ready."

Jacques drove Elise in that infamous red convertible through the streets of Marseille. They drove through winding roads on the outskirts of the city. It made her queasy as Jacques whipped around corners. They went up steep hills and around bends she had been certain were one way (until that other car was coming straight at them). They arrived at a windy private road, reaching the wrought iron front gates of the Marseille Mansion.

Jacques punched in a code on a security system. It included two visible security cameras in place. Who knew how many invisible security cameras were around. Elise eyed the neat rows of cypress trees as the gates opened for them. Their red convertible purred all the way down the tree-lined road. Manicured gardens outlined either side. She heard rushing water.

"Are we near a river?" she asked Jacques over the roar of the engine. Jacques laughed and pointed to their left. As Elise turned, she saw a Versailles-like fountain. Statues, crystals, and marble all competing for her attention. Her eyes widened. "There's a matching set on the other side of the estate," Jacques called to her.

Elise tried counting the number of security cameras she saw on the drive in, but stopped after ten. The mansion came into view. As they turned around a bend, Elise glimpsed at the shiny copper roof. As they got further, she drew an inward breath. If the Disneyland Castle had been a French estate, with a solid dash of Versailles-like charm added, it *might* come close to the grandeur that the Dubonier estate conjured. As a realtor, she had an eye that immediate assessed the details of a house and the monetary value. The roof, the stories, the windows–how big, how updated, how many–the doors, the landscaping. Her realtor-radar was going berserk.

Jacques seemed to clue in on her stupor, as she stared at the house agog. "I know. I felt the same way when I first saw it," he called out over the engine. He came to a full stop in front of the doorway of the semi-circular driveway. In the middle of the driveway was another jeweled fountains. This one had copper and gold accents to match the roof..

"I guess they don't have to worry about neighbors," Elise laughed, as she looked around.

Jacques shook his head. "They own the land for many kilometers or as you would say, for miles and miles. And it gets even better," he said. He opened the car door for her, and she stepped out onto a shiny marble driveway.

She shook her head. "What in the world..."

Jacques jumped in. "Trust me, it will save us both a lot of time if you don't dwell on the details for this first look, or we'll be here for days."

They walked up a marble staircase to the front door. The door handle itself was crystal and gold. It took everything in Elise's power not to whip out her iPhone and start photographing it all in a frenzy. The doorbell chimed and the pair of them waited in the exterior entryway. She did a double take upon seeing the tiny mosaic pieces created the image of doves and swans flying above them on the underside of the roof.

Elise had expected a butler or someone to open up the front door. When the statuesque door opened, Luc stood on the other side. Beside him was a small fluffy dog wearing a silver leather collar, looking up at them with a quizzical expression. It was the same dog from that photo he had sent–the only of him and his "family". The small dog gave a high-pitched bark before trotting away.

"*Bonjour*," Luc greeted them with a wide smile. Her heart skipped a beat when she laid eyes on him. Luc gestured towards the small dog. "That's Joie. Welcome to my home."

It took Elise a moment to register again that this was his *house*. Whenever she had seen him in the past, he had seemed so normal. The stories that Jacques had told her came back to her in a rampage. He had been through so much in the last year. She saw him in a different light now. Still the same Luc, but different somehow.

Jacques stepped inside, leaving Elise out on the front steps.

"Come on, what are you waiting for?" Luc said, giving her a warm smile.

Elise stepped in to the foyer–more marble, more mosaics. Looking up, the roof of the foyer was a glass dome, allowing sunlight to dapple in through the gold-tinged glass. She barely noticed that Jacques and Luc were getting started without her, listing off more facts and figures for her to note.

Elise followed them into the formal living room. What part of this house wasn't formal? she wondered. The kitchen was a chef's dream come to life. Outfitted with twelve gas burners and three enormous ovens, there were even two pizza ovens built into the wall to make wood-fired pizzas. On the adjacent terrace, there was a full outdoor kitchen, built-in barbeque and grill. Even an outdoor wood-fired pizza oven was available. A refrigerator that looked to be the size of a small truck stood upright.

Clad all in white marble, it was also stunning.

"This is my favorite room yet," Elise breathed.

Luc looked surprised. "Really? It never gets used," he said, a tinge of sadness creeping into his voice.

Elise shook her head in pity. "What a shame," she muttered.

The gas range, was begging to boil pasta for dinner, stew tomatoes for lunch, and cook pancakes for breakfast. Continuing on, the rest of the house was more magnificent than she could have imagined. Elise did her best to take it all in without looking too alarmed. There was an indoor pool, complete with a lighting setting that allowed for different views of the stars and planetary alignments depending on where you were in the world. She chose 'Australia', and the constellations changed completely. There was a sauna, a steam room, a gym that was larger than the gym she tried going to in Ashfield a few times a week. There were bedrooms upon bedrooms. Bathrooms with two baths, one bath, and clawfoot baths. Art by famous painters hung the hallways.

"Is that a Matisse?" Elise hissed at Jacques, who gave her a knowing look.

Then there were the outdoor pools–all overlooking the Mediterranean Sea. Her favorite was the waterfall pool. Encrusted with more gold and jewels, it seemed to flow into the sea itself.

"Wow," she breathed. "This is spectacular." She looked around at Luc for confirmation. He glowered instead.

"It's—it's tasteless," he stammered. If it hadn't been his own home, it looked like he would have spit in it. "Who thought to put jewels in a pool? Jewels in a pool?"

She had no idea what that was all about. Up until then, Luc had showed them each room with pride.

"Well, let's move on," Jacques said, casting a nervous glance at Elise and guiding them towards the nearby grill. "What does this do?"

After the entire tour finished in two hours, Elise's feet ached. She was sure she would exceed the ten thousand steps goal she had on her pedometer, just from exploring this house alone. In the final room they visited, the doors opened to the exterior terrace. The room felt airy—almost like an extension of the outdoors itself. She imagined sitting on the sofa there, watching the sun fade along the Mediterranean coastline. It was a spectacular house. She collapsed with great relief into the tufted sofa in what was called the 'family room'. From what Elise could tell, bore no signs that a family had ever lived there. After what she had learned, who could blame Luc for that.

The trio set up a game plan–the following week, they would have an open house. Until then, Jacques had been showing the house only by appointment. So far, there had been no buyers willing to bite off that price tag. An open house in a week was enough time to generate more buzz, but just short enough that people might feel impulsive. They would have to rearrange their schedules and make time to see it. She knew from a psychological standpoint that when something took some extra effort, people typically thought it was more worthwhile. It had to be.

Elise also knew from a home staging perspective, she had a lot of work to do. She understood in part why the home hadn't sold. Yes, it was magnificent. But all the furniture, all the details, screamed that this home was *not* loved. There were no personal touches. Nothing homey or cozy.

"I'll try to arrange for more viewers. It will be tough though," Jacques said. "As I said to Elise earlier, this sale requires a very particular type of clientele. Sure, they're around the Riviera. But they're not all ready to buy right now."

Luc shook his head, looking at the horizon line. "It has to be as soon as possible. I want to get this house sold."

"Okay," Jacques said. "I'll do what I can. Elise, if you run into any billionaires in your travels, or at that fancy hotel you're staying at, send them this way. Now, I'm afraid business calls," Jacques said, checking his phone. "I will see you next week Luc. And Elise, I'll be in touch later today. *Ah non–*" he said, mid-step as he was leaving. "Luc, I gave Elise a ride over. Would you be able to arrange a car to take her back to her hotel?"

"Oh please, that's not necess—"

"I'll give her a ride myself," Luc said, turning to Elise for confirmation. "If that's all right with you." Elise nodded and waved Jacques goodbye, before it was just the pair of them. As Jacques turned to leave, he gave Elise a quick wink that she would have missed if she hadn't been paying attention. That Jacques.

Her heart pounded. Now it was the two of them. Alone.

The sound of the waves crashing on the shoreline nearby was a wonderful distraction. Luc's housekeeper, Marliane, brought them over a bottle of champagne, two glasses, baguette, and a trio of assorted cheese.

"*Merci* Marliane," Luc said, flashing her a radiant smile. As she left, Luc smiled. "She's been with the house longer than I have. I think she started when my grandfather built it." He shook his head and smiled. "She's more a part of the house than I am," he said ruefully. Joie, who had made herself scarce throughout their tour, re-appeared. She took a seat on Elise's foot before falling to sleep. Joie let out a quiet doggy-snore.

Luc laughed. "She likes you. She doesn't like anyone."

Elise smiled and patted Joie on her head, while Joie opened one eye from her slumbers and stared at Elise. "This house–I mean, you have everything you could ever want in the entire world. Right here," she said, shaking her head in disbelief. "You have everything. I mean you even have a choice of pools..."

"Elise," Luc broke in. "I have a lot, yes. I don't take that lightly. Trust me, I don't. But there are still some things you can't buy up with a credit card."

There was an electric moment of silence between them, before Elise cleared her throat and changed the subject. "It's a lot of house for one person," Elise considered. "Where did you live during the past year?" she asked him. She couldn't help but ask, and her heart pounded as she waited for his response.

Luc whipped his head in her direction, his eyes searching her face for signs of understanding. Of knowing.

He knew that she knew. His expression said it all. "Who told you?" he asked.

Elise gave a half-smile and an apologetic head tilt. "Jacques. He let me in on a few details," she admitted.

Luc shook his head. "This place. It's like you can't keep a secret from anyone. But, to be fair, I suppose it is a rather big secret," he acknowledged. "What was your question again? Where I lived the past year?"

Elise nodded. "Yeah. I mean, if you don't want to talk about it, I under—"

"—No, no. I don't mind," Luc persisted. "I should have told you myself, anyway," he said with a sad laugh. "So during that time? I traveled."

Elise's eyebrows shot up. "Where?"

Luc cracked a smile, as he seemed transported in memories. "Everywhere. I was a bit of a vagabond. I left Marseille, Provence, the South of France, everything," he said, waving his hand dismissively. "I needed to clear my head. I've only been back for...less than one week. I came back after my, uh, well... well when everything happened with my father that required my consultation. But after that I was gone again. I arrived pretty much when you did."

Elise understood that feeling of wanting to get away and nodded. "It must be hard for you, being back."

Luc shrugged. "In a way. But it is my home," he said, looking around. "I mean, until the last year, things were good."

"And what about..." She began, before stopping herself. She didn't know how to put it tactfully. She took a deep breath, preparing herself for saying what she wanted. "What about Karina? Do you think you'll ever get back together with her?" After their conversation the night before, she felt comfortable enough with their dynamic.

Luc searched her face. "No. I can say with a firm and absolute no that we are never getting back together." He looked away, out towards the sea. "I haven't spent much time here, since we had our engagement party," he said, steering the conversation back to the house. Elise wanted to ask him more about it, but he seemed tense as it was. "The rumor mill was–*is*–too aggressive."

"How did you get through that?" she asked, wanting to know more. She couldn't comprehend how he was still there. Still in the shape he was. He had pulled off fooling her into thinking everything was okay. Maybe he was. Who knew? What was his secret?

He paused, taking a moment to consider the question. "Well, I drank a lot of this," he picked up the champagne bottle and laughed. Elise joined him, taking a sip of her champagne. It felt good as the afternoon heat drifted in from outside. "I kind of hauled up for the first few months. I didn't talk to anyone. Not my step-mom, or former step-mom I mean..."

Elise nodded. "I understand." He gave her an odd look before she clarified. "I mean, I don't understand. But I get that feeling of needing space to yourself. Time to recover."

"Gerard helped me out a lot."

Elise tilted her head and frowned. "Gerard Remieux? From Ashfield?"

Luc nodded. "He suggested I come out to Ashfield. Clear my head. Get back in the game. Start doing something again."

Elise raised her eyebrows. "And that's when you looked me up?"

Luc laughed. "I had to do a background check. You have no idea how paranoid I got. People were coming at me, left, right and centre, trying to get me to sell this, buy that..." He shrugged. "I get it, from their perspective. I was someone who suddenly held all the purse strings, and who had just gone through something traumatic. I was the perfect target," he said with a grin.

"But you didn't do any of that? You didn't make any rash decisions?" Elise pressed.

His expression changed. He skillfully evaded the question. "And now I want to get rid of this place," Luc said, with an accompanying change in his tone. "Everywhere. His memory is everywhere."

Elise smiled. "I should get going," she said, feeling like she had overstayed her welcome already. He stood up immediately. "Oh, don't worry," she added. "I can call a taxi."

Luc shook his head. "No. This city is full of crazy drivers. I will drive you myself."

Guilt flooded her as she moved her foot, waking up Joie from her happy slumbers. Joie trotted beside her as the pair of them walked out through the house to the side garage. Luc opened up a side door and carefully put Joie inside. In the garage were ten cars parked side by side. Elise did her best to hide her surprise, but Luc seemed to pick up on it.

"I know, I know. It's a bit much," he said with a laugh. "Most of it is my dad's stuff. Or my grandfathers. What can I say? I'm the spoiled brat who inherited it all." A flash of hurt ran across his face before he smiled. Someone had said that to him before. He opened the door to a black Ferrari. "Shall we?"

Chapter Twelve

Luc had dropped Elise off at her hotel. The entire time, she felt like there was an invisible electric current between them. She had so many questions. So much she wanted to ask him. Everything that had happened to him was so recent. Luc had barely had time to process anything himself. Now that he was back home, what was he doing selling such a wonderful place?

"*Au revoir*," he said as she got out, giving her a sad smile. She wondered if talking about everything had allowed any buried emotions to resurface. Back in university she had taken a few psychology courses. She felt like she knew what she was talking about.

Back at the hotel, Elise had big plans the rest of that day, but none of them involved work. She had already done some shopping and exploring. Now, she wanted to know more about the history of that old city. Why were some parts of Marseille so rough, while others so well maintained? What was the history of this colorful Port city?

Luc's passion for history had rubbed off on her. She booked herself a walking tour of the Old Port of Marseille. After dropping off her belongings at the hotel and changing into a more casual outfit with comfier sandals, she set out to meet the tour group. The meeting point for the walking tour was beneath the chrome and mirror-clad structure at the base of the Old Port. Beside it, fishermen were selling their catches of the day. There were tourists like her, looking around in awe at the port. There were hundreds of boats in the harbor–Elise wondered if Luc's father and Karina had ever docked a boat there. She expected not. They had probably wanted to escape somewhere secluded.

Elise was looking for a tour guide holding up a blue umbrella. In all her enchantment with the harbor, she realized she had already circled him twice. A small group was forming around him–some chatting with one another, eager to get started, and some whose eyes were glued to their phones.

Elise approached. "Is this the English-speaking tour?" A few heads from the phone-lookers popped up, before returning their gaze to their devices. The tour guide, a young man with a full beard and cut-off shorts, greeted her.

"Yes, it is!" he said. He didn't have a French accent, she noticed. It was something else. Spanish, perhaps?

"Okay, we're all here," he said, talking into a microphone, and consulting a list. "We have a good group today of people from around the world. We have some Canadians..." Elise looked to a well-dressed young couple holding hands that he had pointed towards. The way they glowed, she presumed they were on their honeymoon. "...we've got Germans..." Elise looked at a family, all wearing study-walking shoes. "...some Brits... and a few Americans today." Elise looked around the group, seeing that two older women and herself were being singled out. She smiled in their direction and she felt herself relax. This was a friendly looking group.

"My name is Santi. I am not a native from Marseille," he began. "I fell in love with a beautiful French girl from Marseille almost ten years ago. And while we didn't last, my love affair for this city certainly has. Can anyone guess where I'm from?"

A few people shouted out Spain, and one confused woman asked if he was from Monaco. Did she mean Morocco? "I will save you some time," he said, laughing. "I am from Argentina. Now, if you will all please follow me, we will walk over to the first stop. It's not far."

As they began walking, the same woman walked over to him and persisted. "Argentina. Is that near Monaco?"

Santi took them all closer to the water. Using lots of hand gestures, every sentence of his seemed punctuated by an exclamation point! His passion for Marseille was obvious. He told them about the Greek settlers in 600 BCE, landing in a rocky Mediterranean cove–where they now stood. How two of the kings–she never could keep them straight–turned it into shipyards. How World War II left the Old Port in complete ruin. How the entire port was re-stored within ten years of the end of the war.

The cycle of birth, destruction, and re-birth seemed to play such a pivotal role in the life of old European cities. She wondered if the same could be said about old European families. And if Luc might ever rebuild himself after the catastrophic year he had endured.

"So Santi," Elise began, sidling up to her tour guide, prepared to pepper him with questions. "How do you like living in Marseille?"

He grinned a broad smile. "Ah, it is perfect. Once you live here, you realize Marseille is the heart of the world."

Elise nodded with enthusiasm. "And you came here for a lost love, you mentioned?" she asked. If he had been that open about it with a tour group, he wasn't sensitive.

"Yes. I'm afraid the Marseillais, they are heartbreakers," he said with a rueful laugh. "Don't tell me you're here for the same reason?"

Elise shook her head. "No. Not really." She could feel her cheeks reddening by the second and Santi laughed.

"You are here for love," he said with a smile, as Elise looked around to see if anyone had heard. But the rest of the tour group seemed enraptured by the architecture and buildings they passed.

"I mean, no... yes... I don't know..."

Santi gave her a curious look and continued by a steep walkway, glancing over at their group to ensure no one had been left behind. "A word of advice," he cautioned, all jovialness gone from his tone. "Love will only break your heart."

Elise swallowed the lump in her throat, unsure how to take his words of caution. "Right," she agreed, nodding.

Elise and the tour group followed Santi along wide roads and down narrow winding streets. He told them the drink of choice in the South of France, and especially Marseille was Pastis.

They passed what looked like a hundred lawn bowling stations in the city. Finally, they stopped at one. "Can anyone tell me what this is?" Santi asked the group.

That same woman, who remained un-chastened by her wrong answers, chimed in. "It's lawn bowling!"

Santi was patient with them, as the other patrons threw out guesses. They were all wrong. "Bocce ball, otherwise known as pétanque, in these parts," he explained. "It is the unofficial sport of this region. Now, don't think that this is a sport just for the old people," he said with a laugh. "When I first came to Marseille, I had never seen this game. But now I have friends younger than me. On a Friday night, we will drink some Pastis. I will want to go out dancing, to a discotheque, but my friends who grew up here..." he shook his head. "They will want to play pétanque all night. And let me tell you, it looks tame. But you haven't seen what drunk men playing this game at one in the morning looks like." He mimed throwing the heavy balls overhand, rather than under. "Some of the worst sports injuries I've seen have come from pétanque," he said gravely.

Elise stifled a giggle. She couldn't imagine a less dangerous looking sport if she tried. But then again, she had never played. Or had Pastis. There was a first time for everything. As she thought that, she heard someone yell something in French.

"Watch out!" Santi called out.

A few people on the tour ducked.

Suddenly, a pétanque ball flew past her head, missing her by a couple of inches. The group was silent for a moment as one of the older men playing pétanque ran over, apologizing to her profusely in French.

"*C'est d'accord*," she insisted. That's okay.

As the older men returned to their game, Santi shook his head. "I have never seen that happen before. You are one lucky woman."

The group was eventually led to Le Pharo. Elise had read about this building. Built as a residence for Napolean, it was surrounded on one side by sculpture-filled park. The park was now a popular picnic spot for les Marseillais, and it backed onto the Mediterranean Sea. The Catalans Beach was nearby, marked by open-air restaurants serving bouillabaisse. Located in what she imagined was the most perfect location, it was a sight to behold. Still, Elise thought back to Luc's estate.

"We will end our tour here," Santi finished, after telling them about the history of the estate. It was now a public building–so no one individual could purchase it. Elise's realtor eyes darted around the palace in that way that they did whenever she saw a gorgeous property.

"*Merci*!" Elise said to Santi, thanking him and providing a generous tip. He smiled back and continued thanking the rest of the patrons. Elise strolled in the direction of Le Pharo. It would have been the most perfect home, Elise thought. Apart from Luc's, of course.

As she drew nearer to the palace, her attention was diverted when she overheard a middle-aged couple. She zeroed in on their conversation.

"...if only it was for sale..."

"...probably seventy million? What do you think?"

"...make an offer in a second..."

Elise cast a glance in their direction. The woman carried a crocodile Hermes Birkin bag, which Elise knew cost well into the six-figures. She beamed. Her obsessions with handbags was *finally* paying off. Unless it was a fake, which was a serious possibility, this couple was *seriously* loaded. It was a risk she was willing to take. The aesthetics of the couple cemented her decision. The woman had thick, shiny hair down to her waist, and the man wore a suit.

She walked over to the couple. "I couldn't help but overhear," Elise began, giving them a friendly smile. The couple peered at her warily.

"Excuse me?" the man said, in a comically deep voice.

Elise wished she had been wearing a smarter outfit at that moment. Her jeans paled in comparison to the woman's ivory silk trousers. "My name is Elise. Elise Laird. I sell luxury real estate. I heard you liked this house. And you, sir," she looked in the man's direction. "You were probably spot-on with your assessment of the property value."

He glimmered with pride. Elise had no idea what the property value was. And neither did they. Luckily for her, as a public property, that information would likely never be disclosed. She knew that flattery was often the key to getting her foot in the door.

"We are the Dominiques," the woman said, extending a manicured hand. Her rings were studded with large diamonds. Elise knew she had been spot on in her assessment of this couple. "My husband Alex, and I'm Clara." Clara spoke with a hint of an accent she couldn't place.

Elise smiled. "It's so nice to meet you both. Now, I know this is highly unorthodox." She pulled out her business card from her purse, grateful to have her purse, Lord, with her at that moment. She knew it was a gutsy move. "But I am selling a stunning home in Marseille. If you like Le Pharo..." she let out a low whistle, as if to signify the importance of this property. "...you will love the property I have to show you. I am working with Jacques at Maison Leveque."

Clara's eyes widened, as she looked to Alex. "We have worked with him before. He sold us our home in Cap Ferrat."

Elise smiled. Bingo. She wasn't sure where Cap Ferrat was, but would look it up later. "Jacques is the best," Elise said pleasantly. "I am afraid the house is fairly expensive," she said, pulling a face. "Just North of what you before had suggested for this home, Alex."

Alex turned white as a sheet. Clara jumped in, seemingly unfazed. "In Marseille?"

Elise nodded. "Just outside. It is truly something else. I have truthfully never seen a home like that before."

The couple glanced at one another. "Who owns the house now?" Alex asked.

"The family likes to maintain their privacy. But I can assure you. If you like Le Pharo, you are in for a big treat."

Elise held out her business card and Clara took her gratefully. "We will be in touch."

Elise nodded. "I wouldn't wait. This house will not be on the market long," she said casually, as Clara cast a nervous glance at her husband. "If you like, I can set up a private viewing for you next week. Or as soon as you like. Of course, with appropriate documents," she said.

Clara hissed at her husband. "Book it. Book it," as Alex pulled out his phone.

"I'll put in a reminder on my phone to call you tomorrow," he said in his deep-voice. She shook each of their hands.

"I look forward to hearing from you both," Elise conceded.

It only took a few hours before Elise had retreated back to her room and ordered room service before her phone rung, revealing a Marseille-based phone number.

"*Bonjour*?" she answered.

"Elise? This is Alex and Clara. We would like to see the property."

Chapter Thirteen

Elise celebrated her small victory that evening by ordering room service. Bouillabaisse and a glass of wine. She ate on the terrace outside her room. The lights of Marseille sparkled below, and the hazy sunset made her feel right at home. Almost like those sunsets back in Ashfield.

Not even forty-eight hours of having been in Marseille, and she had already secured a viewing within two days. She glowed with pride. After Clara Dominique had called her and requested to see the house, Elise had done her due diligence and typed their names into Google to see what came up. She almost shrieked when she realized that they were members of the prominent Dominique family –pharmaceutical-giants and a massive fortune to go with it.

After an early night and falling asleep, Elise woke the next morning to her alarm blaring. Checking her phone, she had two missed calls around 5:00 a.m. and a text message from Luc. A pang of surprise hit her as she opened up the text message.

I need to talk to you. Call me when you get this.

Elise's eyes were still adjusting to the morning light when she hit the call button on her phone.

"Elise?" he picked up on the first ring.

"Hi Luc, what's up?" She sat up in her bed, rubbing the sleepiness out of her eyes.

"How did you get over it?" he asked her. His voice sounded pressured. Intense.

"Get over what?" she asked, feeling more awake at the sound of his voice. She had no clue what he was talking about.

"Your parents. Their, uh, deaths." He sounded exhausted – like he hadn't slept all night.

Elise drew a deep inhale. "Do you want to talk? Why don't you meet me at the hotel for breakfast," she suggested half-hearted, not expecting him to agree to it.

"Okay," he agreed. "I'll be there soon."

It took only half an hour before the concierge rang her room phone, letting her know that her guest had arrived and was waiting in the restaurant downstairs. She had thrown on a white silk halter-top and white jeans, feeling inspired by Clara's outfit she had seen the day before. She just hoped that she wouldn't spill any coffee on herself, as she took the elevator downstairs to the lobby.

"*Bonjour*," she greeted Luc, as she walked into the adjacent restaurant.

He looked even worse than he had sounded on the phone. Dishevelled, with mussed hair and dark circles under his eyes. A deep furrow had developed between his brows since the last time she saw him.

"Thank you for meeting me," he began, giving her the usual kiss on each cheek. She was getting pretty good at it by now. "I'm so sorry to have bothered you. I feel so silly," he admitted. He looked sheepish as he spoke, and Elise cut him some slack.

"That's alright. What's going on?" she asked. They ordered–an almond croissant for her and a cappuccino, a *pain au lait* with butter and jam, and cafe for him.

Luc rubbed his forehead. "Just being back. It's bringing up a lot of stuff."

"Emotions?" Elise asked.

Luc nodded in frustration. "How do you get them to stop?" he asked.

Elise laughed, taking a large bite of her almond croissant. "I don't think you can, Luc. You can't hide from your feelings."

His frown deepened. "Okay, well what did you do? How did you feel *better*?"

Elise didn't know how to respond. She herself didn't know. "Time, I suppose? I threw myself into work. It wasn't what a therapist might propose, but it kept me distracted. It kept me busy."

Elise hated to admit to herself that she wasn't the best person to be asking these sorts of questions to. She had buried herself in work, and obsessed about Rose's wellbeing. It had been one way to channel her emotions.

"Did it help?" he asked, his eyes brightening.

Elise shook her head, feeling like she should have him sign a waiver of some sort, showing that he acknowledged she wasn't qualified to give this advice. "I don't think so. I have a friend back home, Rhonda, who's a psychologist. She always says this one phrase to me. It drives me nuts, but I think it's true. You can't heal what you don't feel."

Luc nodded, a faraway look in his eyes. He repeated in a murmur. "You can't heal what you don't feel."

"I also spent a lot of time at their gravesite. I enjoyed talking to them. I know it sounds rather morbid," she said, laughing. But it had been true. That first year, she had gone more than she cared to admit. It had helped provide her with a fraction of comfort.

Luc frowned. "I haven't been to the grave since the funeral."

Elise shrugged. "I mean, it's not for everyone," she said quickly, knowing how much going to the cemetery had always bothered Rose.

"Perhaps I'll try it," he said with a shrug.

"Maybe just give yourself some time." She wanted to tell him she thought selling his house was a bit of a rash move, considering that he had only been back for such a brief period of time. But she kept that to herself.

"How did you forgive the other driver?" Luc asked.

Her heart pounded in her chest. She swallowed the lump in her throat, taking a sip of her cappuccino. "That was the hardest part," she admitted, her hand trembling. She hoped Luc didn't notice. She had carried that anger with her for a long time. Truth be told, she still didn't forgive the teenager who had just gotten his driver's license and had gone out drinking to celebrate. She expected she would harbour resentment towards that driver for the rest of her life.

She knew that feeling was dark and dangerous to dwell on. It was a toxic anger she held, kept alive with rumination. She said words she never thought would come out of her mouth. "Forgiveness is the only way to heal." She exhaled a bit sigh of relief, just saying the words aloud. She knew it was true.

Luc's expression clouded over. "I see."

The two of them finished their coffees in silence. All around them, happy tourists and families were filling up the tables around them. She was certain no one else was having these kinds of conversations.

Luc cleared his throat as he got to his feet. "*Merci*, Elise. This has given me a lot to think about. You know, there are not too many people I feel I can talk to about this. No one actually," he said with a sad laugh. "I should get going. I don't want to take up any more of your day."

Elise stood up. "Oh, my pleasure." She wasn't sure what kind of protocol followed that level of help. Perhaps she should make a joke about being a therapist? One glance at Luc's brooding face told her that was a bad idea. "I'll see you tomorrow. I will come by and do a little home staging. I have a prospective buyer. Do you mind if we start the showing the day after tomorrow? I know it's soon, but I'll be there tomorrow to set up and do all of the staging," she told him. "Around ten in the morning tomorrow? If that works."

Luc nodded but he looked lost in thought. "Sure, sure. No problem." He left without doing the double kiss she had become so fond of. Elise did her best to shake it off and get on with the rest of her day. She walked over to the nearby Maison Leveque office.

Since she was already awake, she figured that now was as good of a time any to get started with work. It's what she should have been doing anyways. She walked through the narrow streets of Marseille, arriving at the Maison Leveque office where Jacques sat beside a huge Apple desktop computer screen. The entire office, although in an ancient building, was modern and minimalist. Everything was white. The only accent colour was the small replica of Jacque's red vintage convertible, which sat on his desk.

"*Bonjour* Elise," Jacques said, without glancing up from his computers. "There are no buyers in this market," he complained.

Elise set Lord down on his desk and took a dramatic pause. "I have a buyer," she announced.

Jacques scoffed. "Oh yes? Who? You?" He still hadn't taken his eyes off of his computer.

"I met them yesterday. Alex and Clara. I believe they said their last name was Dominique," she said, hoping that he would remember their name from his past sale.

Jacques finally looked at her, mouth agape. "The Dominiques? You are sure that was their name?"

Elise nodded. "They said you sold them their home in Cap Ferrat last year. Which, after I looked it up, seems like a nice place." She had looked it up. Saint-Jean-Cap-Ferrat was a nearby destination for international millionaires, between Nice and Monaco on the French Riviera.

Jacques shook his head in disbelief, muttering something that sounded a lot like *beginner's luck* under his breath, which Elise chose to ignore.

"I didn't know they were still looking. I just sold that home to them last year. And they want another? So close?" he persisted.

Elise shrugged. "Who knows. Either way, I told them I would give them a private tour in two days. I will head to the house tomorrow to get it staged and prepped. Not that it needs *much* work," she added. "But it doesn't feel like a home. All sparse and cold."

"Okay. We need to bring in the photographer once you're done staging. Perhaps tomorrow after you're finished?"

"No problem," she said, as Jacques eyes fixed on the screen again. "Mind if I get a bit of work done here today?" she asked. She could use the business centre at the hotel. But working alongside someone was always more fun. She also found she worked more with someone there to keep her on track.

"That desk is all yours," Jacques said, pointing towards a desk on the other side of the office. As she got closer, she realized that in the clear vase was a small bouquet of white tulips, a stack of white pens, and even a full jar of white mints. It was like he had been waiting for her all this time.

She smiled to herself, knowing that while Jacques played it cool, he clearly enjoyed the company too. She parked herself there for the rest of the afternoon, writing up a draft contract, and finishing up marketing materials for the sale. "It's all about the details," Joe had taught her about luxury sales. To that effect, on her way over, Elise had passed by a handmade paper shop, with stunning, one-of-a-kind pieces of paper.

If that didn't scream luxury, Elise didn't know what did.

She had purchased ten pieces of paper–a thick, creamy paper with mottled flecks and real Provençal flowers pressed into the corners. She would give one piece to Clara, one to Alex, and then she would still have a few remaining for mistakes. Or to have on hand. She never could tell when a nice piece of luxury paper would come in handy.

She had no use for fancy stationary before, but she was in the South of France now. The standards could be different. She didn't want to make the mistake of using ordinary paper if the standard in an extraordinary transaction was extraordinary paper.

When Elise told Jacques about the paper idea, he had burst out laughing. It turned out that paper standards were universal.

The rest of the afternoon and evening passed uneventfully. She enjoyed her stroll home from the office, imagining what it must be like to live in a city where each building was more beautiful than the next. Where French was spoken all around her. There was an unmistakable, invisible energy that buzzed all around. She enjoyed taking herself to a small bistro for dinner, ordering *moules marinière* served with garlic, onion, and *herbes de provence*. She slept well and felt rested when she woke up the next morning.

After she was up and risen, it was now her turn to give Luc a call. It went straight to voicemail. She gave him another call and it happened again. It was already half passed nine, and Elise wanted to get everything staged and ready to go. She had brought with her a few vases, throws, and carpets which were everywhere on Pinterest those days, and threw it into a suitcase with wheels. About to call down to the concierge to book a taxi, she remembered Mario's offer. Pulling out his card, she gave him a quick call. As soon as he answered, she knew she had the right person.

"Hello, Mario? It's Elise Laird. I was wondering if you could give me a drive..."

Within minutes, Mario had whizzed up to her hotel and was packing her suitcase into the trunk again. This time, she wasn't leaving home–she was trying to create one somewhere else. "Don't worry, don't worry," he insisted, hoisting the heavy luggage. "I will do it."

Elise took her previous seat up front. As he sat beside her, she gave him the address to Luc's house. "I'm doing a bit of home staging today," she told him. "To get it ready to sell."

Mario nodded. "No problem at all," he beamed. "Today, *madame*, I am at your disposal." He tipped a fake hat, making Elise laugh.

She sat up front with Mario, as he whizzed between parked cars and turning cars, just like last time. As the car ahead of them came to a stop, he threw up his hands in the air. "You see? Be careful driving in this city." He shook his head at the car ahead of them.

The pair of them arrived at Luc's estate. Elise got out of the car and punched in the access code given to her by Jacques the day before. As the gates swung open, Mario raced down the elegant road.

"Nice house you are selling," he remarked, taking in the jewelled fountains with an unreadable expression.

As they approached the front door, Elise got out herself. "Thank you so much Mario. I'll need a lift back home, if you have time."

"Don't worry. I'll be here." Mario smiled and pulled out a newspaper from the backseat, as he pushed his chair back.

Elise smiled, thanked him, and walked up to the front door. She rung the doorbell once and heard the familiar chimes. Unlike the first time she had arrived at the estate, no one came to the door right away. She rang the bell again.

"Where are you," she muttered under her breath, as she tried Luc on his phone again. It went straight to voicemail.

Marliane opened the door. Her tense face eased when she saw Elise. "Is Luc with you?" Marliane asked her, a hint of panic in her voice.

Elise turned around, looking around. The only other person nearby was Mario, who looked enthralled with an article he was reading. She turned back to Marliane and shook her head.

"He's not here?" Elise asked, as if for confirmation, as Marliane wrung her hands.

"Mr. Dubonier is away on a trip," Marliane began, eyes darting from side to side, clearly accustommed to covering up whereabouts. She was fooling no one. Joie turned a corner and ran towards the open door, jumping up on Elise. Given Joie's enthusiasm, Elise felt grateful the small dog could only jump up to her knees.

After Joie lost interest and wandered back inside, Elise crossed her arms. "Marliane. Come on. I know he's not here. What's going on? I'm here to stage the house. The photographer is coming in an hour. I have people we're showing the house to tomorrow. Can I come in?"

Marliane nodded, eyes wide. "I see. I see," she said, biding for time. "Well, the thing is..." she fumbled, wringing her hands further. "...Mr. Dubonier does not like guests in the house when he is not here..."

Elise almost threw up her hands in frustration, and instead took a deep breath. "Okay. Do you have any idea when he will arrive home?"

It was clear from Marliane's expression that she did not.

"Okay then. If Luc shows up, *please* ask him to call me. It's Elise," she said, extending a hand to Marliane. "I can imagine this must be stressful for you. Not knowing where he is."

Marliane smiled and Elise turned around, preparing to walk back to the car. Halfway, she heard Marliane call out after her.

"Wait!" Elise turned around, and Marliane was walking towards her, her eyes darting around the driveway, as if Luc might pop out at any moment. "How well do you know Luc?" Marliane asked.

Elise wasn't sure how to respond. "I'm–I'm not sure. Not all that well, but I mean, I know that he's had a bit of a rough year," she said, trying to lighten the mood. Marliane remained resolute with her serious expression.

"The last time that Luc disappeared," she said, her anxiety plain from a mile away. "He did not come back for six months. I know he's not my son, but well, I worry."

Elise's heart softened. Marliane wasn't trying to cover anything up. She was scared for Luc. Now the question was, *why*? Elise frowned.

"What? You think Luc's gone? I just spoke with his yesterday. He's planning on selling the house."

Marliane shrugged. "That's what he said before he left the last time, too."

Elise felt shaken, but did her best to maintain her composure. "Don't worry, Marliane," she said with her most sincere forced smile. "I'm sure he'll turn up soon."

Chapter Fourteen

Where was he? There was no way that Elise was leaving Marseille without selling that house. She got the impression that Clara and Alex were not people who tolerated being rescheduled. Elise tried calling Luc's cell phone again. Six more times. Each went straight to voicemail. It was now past noon, and Elise was growing wary. She already had to send the photographer home. Her thoughts immediate went to every worst-case scenario. Had someone kidnapped him? It wasn't out of the realm of possibilities. He was a Dubonier, which was as good as being royalty in these parts. Considering France's history, members of their royalty ended up having a rough ride. She called Jacques, letting him know that she would cancel their meeting that day.

"Why?" he asked.

"Something has come up. It's important. Don't worry. I'll meet with you tomorrow. And again–*don't worry*. Have you spoken to Luc, by any chance?" she asked, trying to sound casual.

"No, I haven't. Why?"

She wished he would stop asking that. "He's not here yet. I'm sure he'll be here soon." The last thing she wanted was to create panic.

"At your scheduled appointment?" Jacques asked sounding surprised. "*Very* unlike him. When he has any scheduled meetings with me, he is always very punctual."

It didn't make Elise feel much better, considering what Marliane had said about him being a flight risk, and everything he had told her the day before at breakfast. If there was anyone who seemed like he might be ready to bolt, it was Luc.

"I'm going to figure this out," she said, rubbing the crease between her brows. "I'll just have to catch up with you tomorrow at the showing." *If* there was a showing, she thought.

"Okay. But you owe me, Elise," Jacques said. "Two glasses of pastis and at least one appetizer," he told her. "I had our lunch plans all set up."

Elise laughed, as best she could amidst her worry. "Okay. You pick the place and text me. We can celebrate tomorrow after the successful showing," she said, doing her best to mask the concern in her voice. He seemed to buy it, and said goodbye soon after.

She hung up, feeling relieved to have that conversation out of the way, and disconcerted by what she had learned. Always punctual to meetings? Jacques had been working with Luc for months to sell this house. They had met on multiple occasions. It didn't provide Elise with a great deal of confidence.

Now it was time to figure out what was going on. She had been standing outside of Luc's estate, Mario waited all the while. He had taken to going for a stroll through the estate. Truth be told, he seemed to enjoy his work more than she did at that moment.

Elise walked back up to the front door. As Marliane opened it, Elise came out and said it. "Marliane. I have a client coming tomorrow. I don't know Luc very well, but this is important. Who can I contact who might know where he is?"

Marliane turned around and left almost as quickly as she had opened the door. Elise shook her head in exasperation. Was anyone else going to help her? She returned with a ripped piece of paper. Scribbled on it was a name, phone number, and address. "This is the information for Annette Dubonier," Marliane whispered.

Elise looked at the name and information, written in perfect handwriting. "Who is Annette Dubonier?"

Marliane shifted from one foot to the other. "His stepmother. Or former stepmother... I'm not sure where things were left..."

Elise acknowledged that this was outside of Marliane's comfort zone. "Thank you. I can't thank you enough," she said. "So, should I call her?"

Marliane tilted her head from side to side. "It's possible she'll pick up. I haven't been able to reach her since, well... since everything changed," she said. Marliane was putting on a brave face for Elise, but she could see in her eyes that the past year had been hard on her too.

"I'll tell you what. If I don't reach her by phone, would you like me to check up on her?" Elise looked at the address. It was in Saint-Tropez, an exquisite beach town on the French Riviera, known to be filled with even more beautiful people.

Marliane's face lit up before falling. "Oh, I couldn't ask you to do that."

Elise shrugged. "What else do I have to do? I can't get in touch with Luc, and maybe his stepmom will have some idea."

Marliane looked like the picture of joy as she thanked Elise, and Elise thanked her.

As Elise stepped into the car, she began. "Look, I don't know how much time you've got today. But I'll pay you well. I need to get to this address in St. Tropez."

Elise held her breath, expecting him to tell her he was busy. But Mario shrugged. "*Certainement*," he said. He revved the engine twice. "*J'adore* St. Tropez."

She punched in the address that Luc's stepmother had given her earlier into her phone's GPS, and Mario drove off.

Staring into her phone Elise said, "We should go north to get to the A7."

"What do you mean? You want to tell me, a native Frenchman how to drive? When we are in a hurry?"

"No. It's not me. It's the GPS that has the fastest route mapped"

"Oh, and when was that data recorded?"

"Well, I don't know," she admitted. "But it's always worked for me."

"I follow my instincts as any good countryman should. No computer will ever be better than someone who has the nose for directions. And who knows how to drive."

The GPS predicted a two-hour drive east from Marseille to St. Tropez along A7 and A8. But Mario disregarded the GPS, instead taking her along back routes he insisted were faster.

"You know, Elise, technology isn't everything," he told her, as he made a sharp left turn that had her hanging onto the door handle. They listened to the radio most of the drive there, which fluctuated between American top hits and French discotheque songs. Along the way, he told her all about his life outside of driving.

"I am a painter," he told her, whipping out his phone and handing it to her. She swiped through a series of paintings he had taken pictures of, and drew a breath.

"You did these?" she asked Mario, for clarification. "They're stunning." Elise continued to look at the images of the paintings he did–large, colourful brush-strokes filled the oversized canvasses.

He beamed with pride. "I paint Marseille. Vibrant. Colorful. Never ending energy," he said.

Before becoming a realtor, Elise had at one time considered a career as a gallery curator. To date, she continued to believe that she would have loved working in the art world.

"Well, you're fantastic," she told him. "We've got to get your work into the houses of the clients we're selling to."

As Mario continued to talk to her about his painting style and favorite spots in the city to work, Elise kept her GPS on. It kept beeping and refreshing its map as Mario improvised and changed the route. The estimated time of arrival kept shrinking as they drew nearer to their destination. Despite Mario's maniacal driving style, the journey was coming close to the two hours as predicted. As they drew nearer to Saint-Tropez, the GPS finally came in handy. Mario began to lose his confidence once they were close to their destination.

"Where am I going at this roundabout?" Mario asked in a panic, as cars sped passed them.

Mario circled two times before Elise could call out, "This one! No you missed it. Circle one more time."

The next roundabout came up fast. "What about this one?"

"The first right, no sorry it's the second, there's five exits on this one." Too late. Mario had already exited the first right and had to double back.

They continued on with routines more or less similar for another two-dozen roundabouts, before arriving on the last stretch of the journey.

"Mario, I thought you knew all the roads in France." Elise teased.

"Well I can't be expected to know every little foot path you want me to follow."

They got there in one piece, which was all Elise cared about.

"You see," Mario told her, looking at his car clock. "It is always faster to take the back roads."

Elise laughed. Even with all the mis-directions they had shaved off four minutes from the estimated arrival time. She felt had lost years of her life on those roundabouts.

They pulled up to a beige stucco Mediterranean-style home with palms and olive trees in the front lawn. A well-maintained grey stone garage stood to the left, and vines hung from the Juliet balconies.

It took Elise some nerve to walk up the cobbled pathway leading to the front door before she knocked. There was no doorbell in sight. The door swung open.

"*Bonjour*?" the woman asked. Elise took her in. She was *stunning*. With chestnut coloured hair cropped above her shoulders, a flawless tan, perfect skin, and an impeccable outfit. She couldn't be older than forty.

Elise cleared her throat, attempting to speak French as best she could. She asked the woman if she was Madame Annette Dubonier. Annette asked who was asking. Elise gave her an overview of her relationship with Luc–how she had viewers coming to see the house the following day. How she needed to know if she had been in contact with him. And, how Marliane had wanted to check-in on her.

As soon as she mentioned Marliane, Annette stepped back and invited her into the house, switching to English.

"I can tell by your accent you are not a native. English will be much easier and please call me Annette." She said as she led Elise into the orange-tiled, open-concept living room. "Please, take a seat."

Elise did as she was told, sitting and being absorbed by an overstuffed and squishy white cotton couch. The aesthetic was inspired by the region. Dried lavender hung in bundles from the ceiling. The ceramic coffee table had on it fresh thyme and marjoram growing in white stone pots. Like many French homes, there was no air conditioning. At least, not in use. Instead, cream linen drapery flapped in the wind as the back French double-doors remained open to the backyard, where Elise saw a small olive grove.

It was a Provençal dream house.

"Annette, I am so sorry to interrupt your day," Elise began. "But I'm afraid that I had an appointment with Luc today. He hasn't been answering his phone. Marliane told me she was worried about him. He has had a track record of up-and-leaving, as I'm sure you know..."

Annette looked unfazed. "Perrier?" she asked. Elise nodded, and Annette left to the kitchen before returning with a large glass green bottle, beads of cool condensation already forming on the bottle, before pouring it into two glasses for them.

"*Voila*," Annette said, handing Elise a glass. "So, you are worried about Luc?" she asked, taking a thoughtful sip. Elise nodded. "And, pardon my forwardness, you are, uh, dating my step-son?"

Elise, who had just taken a sip of her Perrier, nearly spat it out. "No, no no no," she said, shaking her head. "I mean, not that I wouldn't want to date, uh, Luc. I mean, he's very handsome and everything," she said, words tumbling out of her mouth before she stopped herself. "But, uh, you know how it is," she said, with an apologetic shrug. She was certain Annette *didn't* know how it was. She exhaled with relief that Annette didn't press her further.

Annette looked amused. "Yes, Luc has a track record of running away from things," she agreed. She surveyed Elise from top to bottom with an unreadable expression. Elise sat up straighter. "It's good he has someone who seems to care about him so much."

"So, do you have any idea where he might be?"

Annette let out a laugh that rung through the house. "No, no I'm afraid not. Luc and I, although not related by blood, are more similar than you would think." Elise nodded, not sure where Annette was going with that. But Annette continued. "After my husband left me for Luc's fiancé, I ran away –"

Elise did a double take, shaking her head in surprise. Perhaps Annette had confused her words. English wasn't her first language after all. "Wait, hold on. What? What did you just say?"

Annette looked taken aback as she repeated herself. "Luc and I are similar..."

"No," Elise jumped in. "The other part. The other part."

"How Luc's father left me for Luc's fiancé?"

Elise felt her heart sink into her stomach. She had understood. "Yes," she said. "Yes, that one."

Elise sat and listened for the next fifteen minutes as Annette provided her with an unfettered, unrestrained account of what had happened that past year. How Luc had announced his engagement to Karina. How he seemed to be coming into his own, Annette said, and even seemed to toy with leaving the Dubonier Company for a while to learn some other skills. But as soon as he had had those kinds of conversations, Annette had watched as Karina grew less enamoured with Luc. "It was obvious," Annette told her. "That tart had no depth.

What you saw was what you got." Annette continued to explain that at their engagement party, held at the Dubonier estate, Annette had walked in on her late-husband being, uh, well, *intimate*, with Luc's fiancé, Karina. She had stormed out in a fit of rage. But there was still a party underway. And she had always hated scandal, Annette explained. She excused herself from the rest of the party and vowed to speak with Luc, her stepson, as soon as possible. His world was about to be shaken.

Annette described the moment that she told her stepson. She had checked into a hotel the night of the party, and had met him at a nearby restaurant for lunch the following day. He hadn't believed her, storming away instead, and saying some regrettable words. She pulled a face, as if recalling that conversation brought back a sea of pain. No sooner had Luc left before he drove back to the house and he caught the two of them red-handed in the pool. They had gotten careless with their affection.

"Not the jewelled one? With the waterfall?" Elise asked, and Annette nodded. She had a flashback to Luc's reaction to it back when she had first seen the house. Was it *tasteless* that he had called it? She now understood Luc's reaction when she had told him it was her favorite. Annette continued to tell her that the rest of the painful story. Luc and Karina had called off their engagement. Luc's father and Karina had set sail on their largest yacht–a failed attempt to escape the local gossip. Luc had left too. He couldn't stay in that house, Annette told her. She hadn't known where he went, only that he was no longer in France. She had tried reaching him again and again. Even though she wasn't his birth mother, she had known him since he was what, ten? Eleven? She loved him all the same. Elise nodded, swallowing through a lump that had developed in her throat.

"And then Luc's father, he died?" Elise prodded. Annette's eyes flashed with pain, before she continued. A heart attack, she explained. While he and the trollop were at an opera in Zürich.

Elise's eyes narrowed.

"Don't worry," she said, her eyes sharp. "They brought his body back to France, where an autopsy was conducted. There were no signs of poisoning or any malfeasance like that..." she said, hurt flashing in her eyes. "...he just sat there at the opera house, lurched forward in pain, and died. They attempted resuscitation drove him in an ambulance to the hospital but he was, as they say, dead on arrival. So sudden, we..."

Elise had no suitable response, and sat in stunned silence with wide eyes instead. Annette shrugged. "What, you can't expect anyone to not have thought the worst?"

Elise gave a feeble smile. She had thought she knew what was happening. She couldn't have been more wrong.

"So where do you think he is now?" Elise asked.

Annette shook her head, averting her gaze. "I don't know. He hasn't returned my phone calls since all of this happened. It has been months since we've talked." Annette's eyes became glassy in the sunlight, and she grabbed for a tissue. "*Pardon*," she said, as she dabbed at an errant tear.

Elise shook her head in fascination. Her emotions were so overwhelming that she found her own eyes were most than a little misty. Not from sadness, but from seeing the awfulness of their situation. "I'm so sorry about all of this. I didn't mean to pry," she said.

Annette looked at her with a kind expression. "You know, it's a relief to have someone to talk to about it. I haven't said much to anyone at all."

To Elise, it clicked now when Annette had mentioned how alike she and Luc were. Like stepmother, like stepson.

Chapter Fifteen

Elise left Annette's house a few hours later. After their tear-filled conversation, she had helped Annette pick the olives from her backyard and make some olive *fougasse*—a Provençal-style bread. By the end of their time together, the two women were laughing and smiling together in the kitchen. Elise herself felt a pang of sadness when it came time to leave. If she had been correct in her assessment, Annette looked to be experiencing the same thing. They exchanged their information and pledged to be in touch with each other. If nothing else came of this adventure, at least Elise had made a friend out of this one meeting. Elise left and promised to call if she heard anything about Luc's whereabouts, and also told Annette to call Marliane. Annette had promised she would.

She still had trouble wrapping her head around all that had happened to that poor Dubonier family in the last year, with Annette and Luc left to pick up the pieces. She tried Luc's cell phone again. It went straight to voicemail. As she walked down the street, after sending Mario a text that she was finished, she received an incoming call. Her heart skipped a beat. Luc? As she looked at her phone, it was from number she hadn't seen in days.

"Hi Rose," Elise answered. "What's up?" Elise heard muffled sobs through the line. As if things couldn't get dramatic enough. "Calm down," she said to her younger sister. "What on earth is wrong?"

Rose hiccupped through the line and blew her nose before speaking. "I got fired from my job."

Elise was too stunned to speak and stopped in her tracks. "Fired?"

"Uh huh. They've got this quota system. They told me I wasn't getting enough sales. No one was buying the credit cards or lines of credit from me," Rose wailed.

All of the protective, maternal instincts in Elise kicked in. "Are you kidding? That's horrible. Did they even train you properly?"

Rose sniffed into the phone. "I'm fine. I'm okay. Yeah, I guess they trained me. But, I don't know. I started speaking to other students when we set up those sales booths, and I guess I never stuck to the sales script."

Elise's interest piqued. "What did you end up saying?"

There was a momentary pause and Rose blew her nose. "I don't know. I guess I talked to them a lot about getting a credit line in a responsible manner. I told them about what happened to me. I asked them if they really needed it..."

A warm feeling spread over Elise. "Oh, Rose..."

"I know, I know. I should have stuck to the script. Then, I'd still have a job –"

"—No!" Elise interjected. "I'm so proud of you, sweets. You stuck to your guns. You stood your moral ground. I'm way prouder of you for doing that than if you had continued at a job you hated."

"Really?" Rose asked.

"Yes. Absolutely," Elise responded.

Rose let a giggle escape, followed by more tears. "When they fired me, I found out that the guy they teamed me up with this guy who was hired a week earlier... he snitched on me." Another giggle came through the line. "I guess I got a little heated. I was talking with a student right out of college, already carrying a student loan who wanted a credit card just so they could go on vacation and not worry about expenses. I asked them if they wanted to die in debt. I mean, I just wanted them to be cautious! I think the exact words my boss particularly didn't like was when I uttered the 'graveyard of debt' bit."

Elise wanted to laugh, but it sparked something in her she never would have come to otherwise. *Graveyard...*

"Rose, I've got to go. I'm prouder of you than I ever have been and even prouder to be your sister. Keep me updated if you get any more information about what's going on. Love you."

"Will do. Love you too," Rose sniffed.

Just as Mario pulled up, rolling his window down, Elise ran over. "Mario, do you know where the Dubonier plot is? Is there a cemetery in Marseille?"

Mario pondered for a moment. "The Cimetière Saint-Pierre is a good bet. It is the largest cemetery in Marseille," he said. Elise nodded. It wasn't much of a lead, but it was worth a shot.

Mario and Elise reached the cemetery within less than two hours flat. Elise kept her GPS turned off this time, trusting that Mario would get them there in one piece. They parked along a graffiti lined road with low stonewalls.

"You want me to come with you?" Mario asked, but Elise shook her head.

"Thanks so much, Mario. I think I will try this one on my own."

"As long as you're paying me by the hour, you can take as much time as you want." Mario teased.

"You're the best."

Elise walked through the gate along a meticulous and well-maintained road. Alongside her, to her right and left, were imposing grey stone mausoleums and tombstones as far as the eye could see. She walked into the visitor's centre, which was empty except for an ancient grounds-keeper sipping a cup of coffee with a newspaper on his lap. She asked him if he could help her locate one particular tombstone. The man didn't say much when she asked about the name, only looking it up in the system, and providing her with a map, drawing the outline of where she had to go. "You have little time. Half an hour. *C'est quatre-heur et demis*. We close at five," was his frank dismissal of her.

"*Merci*," she thanked him, and he nodded his head and returned to reading his newspaper.

Elise persevered past the monuments placed side by side. The hubbub of Marseille's busy streets faded into the distance the further she walked. The sound of cars honking was replaced with silence and the wind rustling through the trees. Elise took a deep breath, enjoying the summer air. The golden sunlight poured down on her in a way she had never seen replicated outside of Provence.

A drop of self-doubt emerged as she continued down the road, doing her best to follow the directions on the winding paths. Perhaps this was just a wild goose chase. She stopped dead in her tracks.

Ahead of her was a giant mausoleum. Accented with copper and jewels. Elise had seen that design before. It was distinct. Unforgettable. She didn't need the map to tell her where she was going. Elise walked in stride to the mausoleum, only a short walk away from the main path. As she drew nearer, she heard a familiar voice from within the building. *Luc*. Elise quickened her pace, her heart racing. She had been right. She was *right*. Almost as quickly as she had hurried did she stop, as another voice chimed in. This time, a woman.

Elise couldn't hear what they were saying, and she felt a pang of uneasiness wash over her. As she took a few steps closer, she glimpsed where the voices were coming from. The gate and door to the mausoleum were open, and from it came the echo-y voices. Elise took a step back, careful she would get caught spying. She didn't mind if she had come across Luc on his own. But Luc and another woman?

She feared what he would think of her. Would she become a running joke?

Just as two figures exited from the Dubonier mausoleum, Elise busied herself by fixing her gaze at a nearby headstone. *Jean-Pierre Lacroix. 1843 -1901*–it read. Elise fixed her gaze on those faded numbers as the voices became louder. She allowed herself to peek in their direction, not daring to move her head. Luckily for her, they seemed enraptured in conversation.

She spotted Luc. Luc–with his rumpled hair, dark jeans, and tucked in button-down. He looked irritated from the way he made slight jerky motions as he spoke. Even more interesting to Elise, though, was the stunning blonde woman he was talking with. With hair down to her waist and a light blue sundress, Elise wasn't sure about who she was. She was close enough to catch snippets of their conversation.

"...Karina... *non, c'est pas vrai...*" Luc was saying. Karina. Karina. Elise did a double take of the woman, who now had her hand rested on her hip. She looked every bit the temptress that Elise had imagined her to be. Elise knew that she should try to walk away. But she worried that if she began moving at all, that she would draw attention to herself. Now that she knew the woman standing with Luc was Karina, the father's mistress, the centre of all the misery in this family, well, her curiosity got the better of her.

"...Luc, I'm sorry..." she heard, as Karina's voice rose. She strained herself to hear what was being said, all the while cursing the birds that were making a racket above her in the solid old trees.

Before she got to hear anything else, she felt a sinking feeling in her stomach, as she watched Luc lean over and give Karina a kiss.

Noooooooooooooo—she felt herself scream in her mind. She took that moment as they were together to turn and walk away, which quickly turned into a run. Discarding the map, Elise didn't have time to remember which direction she had come from. As she turned to make her escape, every row in the graveyard looked just like every other row. Worrying she was about to run around in circles, from behind her, she heard her name being called.

"Elise? Elise?"

A cold shiver ran through her. She stopped in her tracks. She contemplated continuing to run-walk, but her feet stayed in place as soon as she heard her name. It was like her feet were betraying her head, which was telling her to run. To get out of there.

Instead, she turned, plastering a fake smile and attempting a look of surprise. "Luc!" she said a few octaves higher than usual. "What a surprise!"

She was fooling no one. Luc looked at her with an incredulous expression. "What are you doing here?" he asked. Elise scanned the environment. Karina was gone–thank goodness–so at least she didn't have her to contend with. Still, Luc's shock couldn't be more obvious. She would have laughed at his expression if the situation weren't so terrible.

For a moment, Elise contemplated lying. Her breaths were coming in shallow bursts. This hadn't been how she expected things to go. Not that it had been a thought out plan, but still.

The two of them stood across from one another, surrounded by silence and gravestones. He peered at her with an unreadable expression. Elise summoned the courage to respond.

"I was looking to tell you that there are interested buyers," she said primly, smoothing her top. She did her best to maintain an air of professionalism.

Luc wasn't buying it. "You came here to tell me I have a buyer who is interested?" he echoed, his eyebrows raised high on his forehead.

"*Mhm.*" Elise nodded.

"That's all you came here to say? How did you even find me?" he asked, laughing at the ridiculousness of it all.

Elise had always been quick on her feet. She fired back. "Marliane suggested that you might be here," she said, silently apologizing to Marliane. She would make it up to her.

Luc nodded, his brows furrowing as if he was trying to piece it all together. "Oh, okay. Well, I'm glad to hear that there might be a sale in place," he said slowly.

Elise continued and spoke at a rapid-fire pace, the way she always did when she became nervous. "I've told the prospective buyers that they can see the house tomorrow. But I need to come in and stage. There are a few tweaks we still need to make. And the photographer has to come in. They're demanding a specific time when the light is best."

Luc looked far away in thought. "Oh, okay. No problem." He snapped into focus. "Text me when you have a...shoot. My cell phone!" He pulled it out of his pocket. "I forgot to charge it. You haven't been trying to reach me for very long," he asked. "Have you?"

Elise lied through her teeth, as she did with all clients. "Oh no. Not long at all."

Chapter Sixteen

Back at the Maison Leveque office, they could have cut the tension between Elise and Luc with a knife. Had she only imagined their connection in earlier moments? Was she that naive to think perhaps, just maybe, he had liked her? But, he had reconciled with Karina.

How? Elise kept wondering, but she shoved that thought aside.

She should be happy for him, she told herself. She had no claim to him. He was, as far as she knew, still engaged to her. They were putting their differences behind them. No reason they shouldn't. Mistakes get made, people forgive. She had even been the one to tell him to forgive. She would kick herself if she could. Elise reminded herself he was her client. "A *client*, nothing more. I am his realtor, nothing more" She repeated those two sentences inside her head several times to get them to stick to her brain.

The pair of them had agreed to meet back at Maison Leveque to come up with a final sales contract, the only agreement they had up to this point had been verbal, and a list of the fixtures that would be included with the sale, such as the furniture, chandeliers, household appliances. Most important, of course, was the art and sculptures that accented the property. In a usual sale, fixtures comprise used washing machines or a bookshelf that is too much trouble to move out, but this sale was anything but usual.

"Just give it to them. Whatever they want," Luc said, each time a new item was listed.

Elise and Jacques exchanged a knowing glance. "You know, Luc," Elise began. "You might want to consider some of these things. I mean, that artwork..." she trailed off, looking to Jacques for help.

Jacques had a different style with sales. "You know if they want to buy that artwork, let them. We can help brokerage a very tidy deal from it," he said, flashing Luc a mega-watt smile.

Elise glowered. She hated watching this. While she felt jilted by him, sure, she didn't want him taken advantage of. She felt like she too was a vulture. Luc seemed like he couldn't care less about any of the documents. He kept looking up at her, which she did her best to ignore.

Elise cut in. "Well, we can go over all of the terms and details *with specifics...*" she shot Jacques a look. "...*if* the sale is final."

"*Once* the sale is final," Jacques said. "I have a very good feeling about tomorrow," he said, a glint in his eye. Elise forced a smile. "Now, I'm late for my next appointment," he said while checking his watch. "Elise, you'll lock up when you're done?"

She nodded, having watched him do it when she came in the other day. It was a simple process requiring pulling down the metal gate on the outside of the building when they were done.

"Great. I'll see you two tomorrow!" Jacques said, before leaving and hopping into his red convertible that was parked outside.

After the door shut and the rumble from the car engine had faded into the distance, it felt like the tension between them escalated. Elise was quick to respond.

"Well, it seems like we have pretty much everything laid out," she said in clipped tones, eyes fixed on the documents. "I just need your signatures here, here, and here," she said, pointing to a few specific lines. "And we can go over the rest later."

"Elise—" Luc began, his voice softening.

"—Now, if you'll just sign," she cut him off, handing him a pen.

It took Luc a moment before he shook his head and signed. Luc stood in place, his eyes fixed to hers.

"Why were you really there in the cemetery?" he asked her again. Her cheeks burned with humiliation. Elise had been vulnerable. She had told him things she had told no one about her parents' deaths. *He* was the one who hadn't told her the truth about the past year. *He* was the one who hadn't been forthcoming. She didn't understand why now *she* was the one to answer to the honesty police.

Elise averted her gaze. "Like I said, I was there to find you. To tell you about this deal."

Luc dropped his eyes and shook his head. "All right. If you say so," he said.

He gave her the keys to the estate and told her to do what she liked with it. He planned to be out for the rest of the day. Just before Luc left, he said the one phrase that would throw Elise's composure upside down.

As he left, he turned to look at her, like a light bulb had ignited in his mind. "You know, we're not together. Me and her..." before opening the door and walking out, leaving a perplexed Elise in his wake. Her feet were rooted to the floor for just a moment, otherwise she would have run after him, seizing the moment that those words might have signalled. By the time she felt like herself again, he was gone.

The next day was the viewing. Elise had contacted Alex and Clara the day earlier, confirming the time, date, and specific location. Jacques had his banker friend look into their finances upon their consent, and had checked out that they were solvent. "With these kinds of sales..." Jacques had told her earlier. "...you always have to do your due diligence and background checks. You don't want a whole bunch of people curiosity seekers, wasting your time looking at multimillion-dollar properties. And trust me, if you let them, they will."

Elise had kept that in mind and had squealed in delight when she heard that Alex and Clara checked-out regarding their financials. She had been a little worried. *More* than a little. She had lost sleep over it the night before. Now it was full-steam ahead. Go-time.

Elise had the house staged. All family pictures, not that there were many, had been stashed away. It had been de-cluttered, and Elise had made her way to the estate early in the morning to get started. Luc was nowhere to be found, but at least this time Marliane let her in.

Her first stop was in the kitchen, where Elise pulled out a cookie tray – never used. She pulled out a roll of dough she had bought at a nearby grocery store and began cutting it into pieces. Joie made herself at home at her feet, waiting for bits of dough to be dropped. Unfortunately for that little dog, Elise was a very tidy baker. She gave Joie sporadic belly rubs instead.

"What are you doing?" Marliane asked from behind her. Elise nearly dropped they entire tray as she jumped out of her skin.

"You scared me," she said, laughing, before sliding the tray into the oven. "I'm baking cookies. It's my secret weapon for a successful sale," she said with a wink. It only took ten minutes before the entire house, or at least that wing of it, was filled with the smell of warm chocolate chip cookies.

Marliane looked on. "Is there anything I can do to help?" she asked.

Elise turned to her. "You know, Marliane. That would be incredible."

Marliane went to work, adding cozy touches everywhere. While the Dubonier estate was fantastic, magnificent even, the word *homey* certainly didn't apply. "There should be life in every room," Joe had taught her, early on. Marliane had left after with an assortment of fresh flowers, and had busied herself arranging them. She looked pleased with herself, humming to herself all the while. Elise noticed that Marliane was being selective about where to put them. As she passed by a room, she was taken aback by the artful arrangement of lilies, roses, and snapdragons.

Elise put all thoughts of Luc out of her mind, as she fluffed the throw pillows and lit scented candles throughout the home—Tahitian vanilla and Provençal lavender. It always worked like a charm. As she walked through the house, she couldn't help it as her thoughts kept drifting back to Luc. What had he meant the day before, when he said that they weren't together, him and her? Did it mean they were about to get together? Or that he wanted to get together but she was reluctant? She had spent most of the night before trying to work out what it meant, coming to no real conclusion. One thing was certain, Elise had witnessed them kissing. Kissing! He still didn't know that she knew about the, well, *overlap* in family matters, to put it mildly. He still hadn't told her. But then again why would he? They worked together, he was a client, nothing more, she reminded herself yet again.

The house was sparkling clean by two o'clock, when Alex and Clara would arrive. The dining room table was set for what looked like the most picture-worthy Sunday dinner. There were potted plants that had been carefully placed in spots where the sun shone through the windows. They set the arranged flowers on every surface.

"You want to balance clean and lived-in," Joe had taught her, back when she was starting out.

With the Dubonier estate, Elise was doing her best to add personal—but not *too* personal—touches to each room. Flowers, candles and throw cushions often did the trick. They lined the entranceway foyer with about twelve candles and Elise was just lighting the last of them when the silver Bentley pulled into the circular driveway.

"Ready," she said, looking to Jacques and Marliane, who both nodded in agreement. Marliane had been a huge help, ensuring the entire house was spotless. She seemed to enjoy the company and hubbub that prepping for the sale brought with it.

"*Bonjour*!" Jacques and Elise said in union as Clara and Alex, having the car door held open by their driver, stepped out. They all greeted one another in a flurry of cheek kisses.

"All right, shall we?" Jacques asked, giving Elise a quick wink. "You are the very first to have a peak in this exclusive, rare viewing." The couple glowed, pleased to be provided with such an elite tour before they showed the property on the websites to the public.

Jacques pointed out all of the details of the exterior of the house—the roofing, the history, the details. The couple nodded and made happy *mmm* sounds the entire time, sneaking ecstatic glances at one another. Elise handed them each a brochure, with details about the history and home. She had to admit, it had turned out. All cream, and thick handmade paper, with little flowers pressed into the corners. Clara turned it over, examining it in silence.

They stepped into the house, the pleasant aroma of cookies, vanilla, and lavender subtle, but enough to make an impression. Alex and Clara's eyes were wide with wonder, and Elise and Jacques took turns pointing out unique features and touches that the home boasted. For a house of this calibre, it was all about the *non*-essentials. The things that no one needed.

"...chandelier with diamond accents..."

"...jewel encrusted fireplace..."

"...black calacatta marble tiling..."

Once they had arrived at the jewel-encrusted pool, Clara looked like she was sold. Alex played his cards closer to him, his expression giving nothing away. By the time they came back inside and into the kitchen, which now smelled like heaven and had a plate of baked warm chocolate chip cookies on the table, even Alex looked like he was warming to the prospect of waking up in that house.

Elise could feel it coming. They wanted it. Jacques had fussed with his watch, a sure sign that he too, was nervous. Just as Clara opened her mouth to speak, Luc came in out of nowhere. His eyes were alert, taking in all of the subtle changes.

"*Bonjour*!" Luc greeted the guests, giving both of them a kiss on each cheek. "So nice to have you here!" he said. Elise shot a glance at Jacques, who played it cool. What was Luc doing? "What do you think of the house?" Luc asked, gesturing around wildly. "Have you seen the breakfast nook?" he asked them, pointing to the linen-clad booth in the corner. Luc walked over to the table and helped himself to a cookie.

Elise surveyed Luc, ready to jump into the conversation at a moment's notice. Clients were notorious for derailing otherwise successful sales. Alex and Clara peppered him with questions, which he answered like shots fired. Elise had no chance of intervening without seeming rude.

"...and do you have children?" Luc asked them, in a reversal of questioning, looking from one to the other with a smile.

Clara returned his warmth. "Yes. We do. Twin sons."

Luc clasped his hands together like that was the news he was hoping together. "How *parfait*," he said. "How wonderful for this house to yet again be filled with laughter." His enthusiasm seemed almost put on.

Alex and Clara exchanged a funny look, just as Elise shot Luc one of disdain. What was he doing? *Trying* to sabotage this sale?

Alex stepped in. "Well, we have a lot to think about," he said, putting his arm around Clara. "You'll hear from us in a couple of days. Let us know when the house goes public."

Elise nodded. "Will do."

"I'll show you out," Jacques jumped in, and he put on the charm, charm, *charm* as he walked Alex and Clara out, complimenting them on their outfits. The trio left and it was Elise and Luc left alone together once again.

Luc smiled, seemingly unaware of the hostile vibes that Elise was throwing his way. "Well, they seemed nice."

Elise glowered. "Yes. And I think they were about to make an offer."

Luc looked surprised. "Really? Huh, who would have guessed. It looks really good in here," he said, looking around. "Like the home of a real, happy family."

Elise exhaled sharply. She did not understand why Luc was acting the way he was, but was in no mood to figure it out. "Look," she began. "I will keep getting this place tidied up. Unless this couple tells us they want it, we will post it online and on social media to garner interest. That means the photographer will be in within the next few days. So, I know you're still living here," she said, trying to be tactful. "But please, try to keep it looking *exactly* like it does right now."

Luc smiled. "Whatever you say," he told her, and took another bite out of one of the homemade cookies. "Wow, these are good. You make them?"

Elise smiled tensely and nodded, before saying her goodbye and taking off for the night. As she stood waiting for Mario to arrive she took three deep breaths. Mario pulled up a minute later. As soon as she got into the car she screamed, "Men! You are all so infuriating!"

Mario looked back at her through the rear-view mirror. "True. So true." was all he said as he pulled out of the driveway a little more carefully than usual.

Chapter Seventeen

Elise woke up early the next morning. Her business items on hold for the day, she possessed a singular goal–to find the best croissant in Marseille. She was stationed to be in the South of France for just a few weeks longer, and she wanted to explore the rest of the city as best as she could. She wanted to go back to Ashfield feeling like she knew Marseille at least almost as well.

At the rate things were going, she could say she *somewhat* knew the Old Port and the parameter of her hotel. Today, she hoped to improve on that, and the aim of the tastiest croissant was to be the focal point. As she got dressed in a gray silk camisole, black paper bag pants with a tie waist, black flats, and Lord on her arm, she set out.

After Elise consulted her one-and-only guidebook that she had bought at the airport, she decided she would try the neighborhood–or *arrondissement*as she was learning to call it–of La Joliette. On the water, warehouses had been converted into boutiques and restaurants. There was even the nearby Marché de la Joliette, one of Marseilles busiest markets. It was a neighborhood that appealed to Elise–kind of like the Meatpacking District in Manhattan. Gritty roots with new life breathed into it.

As she walked along the waterfront, Elise took pictures of the Chateau D'If—a fortress on a tiny island, in the heart of the Bay of Marseille—for her Instagram. She sent Rose a selfie of her with the fortress in the background. As she made her way to the market, where her guidebook promised her local fruits, vegetables, and homemade jams, terrines, and the holy grail of croissants, she couldn't help but smile in anticipation.

As she drew closer to the open-air market, a familiar face stood out among the crowd. Her guidebook had not prepared her for that. The procession of high-pitched barking cemented it.

"Luc?" she asked.

As he turned to face her, he looked equally surprised. "Elise? What are you doing here?" he asked, as Joie pulled on her leash towards Elise, her small tail wagging so hard it looked like she might fly away. A canvas bag slung over his shoulder was overflowing with fresh produce.

She laughed. "I could ask the same. You didn't strike me much as the cooking type." She reached into his bag and pulled out a bunch of Swiss chard. "Do you even know what to do with this?"

He laughed. "Perhaps you inspired me yesterday," he said, and a warm feeling spread through her, which she did her best to ignore. "Will you join me?" he asked, gesturing towards the row of stalls ahead of them.

Elise couldn't see any reason not–her own frustrations with him notwithstanding. "Sure," she agreed. Ahead of them, rows and rows of umbrella-covered stalls were filled high with fresh pears, apples, plums. There were lemons, oranges, and fresh artichokes. Each stall had the location of where the fruit had been grown, along with the price. She had never seen something like this. Her own local farmers market, held only on Sundays–when the weather held out–paled in comparison.

"I used to come here every week with my dad," Luc began. Elise could hear the tension in his voice as he spoke about it. "He was a wonderful cook."

Elise nodded, unsure how to respond. "What kinds of foods did you make?"

Luc smiled. "Ratatouille. Bouillabaise. Gratins. Real, traditional Provençal recipes," he told her with audible delight. "He learned from his grandfather, who worked these lands. He didn't even speak French. Only Provençal." Luc seemed to catch her quizzical expression and explained. "Until the French Revolution, France was a patchwork of different languages and cultures. There were, and still are, the Basques, the Bretons, the Corsicans, the Provençals.... all different languages, cultures, foods. But when the French Revolution happened..." he snapped his fingers. This momentarily startled Elise, who was listening enraptured by his story. "...when it happened, the entire language of the country changed to the French that it is today. Still, the Provençal remained spoken in these parts, as regional dialects still remain in other parts of the country."

Elise was dumbfounded. "I had no idea."

The creases of Luc's eyes crinkled as he smiled. Elise bumped into a table it caught her so off guard. "My great-grandfather," he continued. "He worked the lands. He sold fruit at markets just like this. Perhaps this very one." They looked around, Elise half expecting some sign to pop up in a twist of fate. But the locals continued the bartering and passer-bys kept on walking. "Then my grandfather, he was the one who changed the history of our family."

Elise watched as Luc changed the subject, asking a vendor in rapid-fire French about where the lemons were from, when they had been picked.

And their price? Too much!

No, the shopkeeper insisted. It was consistent with fair market prices, he insisted. Ask anyone.

Luc agreed, paying the shopkeeper and filling his overflowing bag with three lemons. As they walked away, Luc had a smile on his face. Joie let out a happy bark. "I've missed this."

Elise was surprised. "Why did you try to get that guy to reduce the price of your lemons?" she asked. She would never think of asking a grocer to give her a discount because she thought the price was too high.

Luc laughed. "It is customary here. If you don't barter, well, some shopkeepers, they take offence." He shrugged. "It's all part of the culture."

Elise nodded. Perhaps she should have tried to haggle the price down of her L'Or and D'Or purse. She would try it next time.

"So your great-grandfather taught your grandfather, who taught your dad, who taught you to cook?" Elise asked.

Luc nodded contentedly. "That's right. Not a single daughter in the family," he laughed. "Not that they would have been the ones to do the cooking," he quickly added. Elise laughed and felt herself relaxing in his presence. The two of them walked by each stall, stopping to look at what each vendor offered, before moving on to the next one.

"What happened yesterday? With the sale?" Elise got up the courage to ask him. "I thought you wanted us to sell the house."

Luc looked uncomfortable. "Yes, no. I mean yes. I want you to sell it," he said. "I don't know. I guess it's just a little harder seeing people looking at it than I had imagined."

Elise nodded and changed the subject. "What changed? Why haven't you been back here in so long?" she asked. She knew she was prodding. But there was something about his willingness to divulge information. She thought he wanted to tell her.

Luc seemed to mull things over in his mind before collecting his thoughts. "Well, the last few years were different."

"How so?" Elise asked.

Luc shrugged, taking a seat on a nearby bench. Elise followed suit. "My dad was always obsessed with our family business. With dominating the market. But in the last few years, he became obsessed with expanding into America." He shook his head. "It took over every aspect of his life. I don't know what changed. It was like a light switch flicked in him. I think him and my stepmom were going through a rough patch, or I don't know... maybe their rough patch happened because he had thrown himself into work."

Elise suddenly wished she had asked Annette about Luc's father. She was sure that Annette would have told her. Elise took a deep breath before speaking up. "Annette?"

It took Luc a moment to register he had not yet told her the name of his stepmother. He turned to face her slowly. "How did you know that?"

Elise could have lied and told him she looked it up online. There certainly was enough information on that family that she could have tracked it down. But she didn't want to lie to him.

"Marliane gave me her contact information. I went to visit her," she explained.

Luc's expression changed. "Why would Marliane give you that information? Why would you go visit her?"

Elise wished that she had a better answer for him at that moment. "Well, you weren't picking up your phone. And Marliane was worried about you. She thought you might have disappeared, like last time that you stopped answering your phone. She said you came back six-months later, only once notifying her by email you were safe. Then, she gave me Annette's information. She said that Annette might have a better idea of where you were..."

Luc shook his head. "She had no right..."

"She was just concerned. We all were," she breathed. It was true. Deep down she knew it was. She had gone that extra mile not *just* out of concern regarding her sale. She had been worried about him. "You have a lot of people who care for you, Luc."

Luc exhaled and took a moment to collect himself. "I guess I'm not used to people being worried about me," he intoned. "My dad was great at a lot of things, but, well, parenting wasn't one of them." He allowed himself to laugh.

"Annette told me about Karina," she continued.

Luc's expression gave nothing away. "Oh yeah? What did she say?"

Elise didn't want to say it out loud. Instead, the two of them sat in silence.

"Thanks for watching out for me, Elise," Luc finally said. "I don't feel like I've had that for a long time."

Elise smiled. "Annette really cares about you. So does Marliane. You have people who care, you know."

Luc rubbed at his nose uncomfortably. "You're probably right. I haven't been a very good stepson. Or pseudo-son, to Marliane," he said with a laugh.

Elise was thinking hard about all the people she knew who cared about Luc. "Gerard also cares," Elise fired.

Luc laughed. "Okay, okay. I get it. Yeah, you're definitely right about Gerard. He saved me from some particularly gruesome life choices."

Elise raised her eyebrow. "Oh yeah?"

Luc laughed even harder. "I almost bought a fleet of yachts in Ibiza with the goal of turning each one into a club. And I would be the ship's captain," he told her deadpan.

Elise sniffed as she tried to cover her laugh. She couldn't imagine anything she would enjoy less–being trapped on a boat with drunk people, music blaring, and being responsible for getting them home safe.

"That's when Gerard brought me to Ashfield. He thought it would be good for me to invest my money. I think he truly thought I was about to fritter it all away on yachts. I was rudderless," he said. Elise laughed at the pun. But Luc continued. "It's like since I met you, I've felt like my life has been sailing a little more on course. Less rudderless." He laughed at his own words. "Cheesy, I know."

Elise flushed. She didn't know what to make of all of this. She stood up. "So, while you've got some ruddy wind in your sails, come on," she said. "Show me the rest of this neighborhood."

The two of them continued walking side by side. Elise herself eventually picked up a few items, namely non-perishables, that she could bring back with her in her suitcase.

The two of them walked away from the market and down to a large open space on the water, passed a series of modern structures. "That there is the MuCEM," Luc told her. "The Museum of European and Mediterranean Civilisations. It's worth checking out, if you've got the time before you go..."

Neither of them had discussed her leaving. She put it to the back of her mind. She didn't want to leave. She had just gotten there. But her flight was scheduled for within two weeks.

"Yeah, I'll try to check it out," she said.

"Maybe I can take you," Luc said, stopping on the sideward and turning towards her. His eyes searched her face for something. She wasn't sure what. Elise felt her pulse quickening. He looked so at home there on that port. The way his hair blew in the breeze. The way his skin seemed to glow as the golden light touched it.

"You look at home here," he said simply.

Elise couldn't help but smile at both the compliment and the idea that he could read her mind. He moved a step closer towards her.

Before Luc could say, or do, anything else, words tumbling from her mouth. "What about you and Karina? I mean, I saw you two kiss."

"Karina and I are finished. Remember when you and I had breakfast at your hotel? You told me that forgiveness was helpful to get over this stuff."

"Yes, but I'm not a profess—" she tried to explain.

"—No, I took your advice. It was good advice," he said, beginning to walk. "To find forgiveness within myself I needed to be with my father. I wanted to find some way of feeling I could be with him to make amends. Things with us, well, they didn't end on good terms." He stopped again. This time, they were on a small walkway, with Le Pharo across the small harbor. He jumped up, taking a seat along the stonewall that bordered the sea. He patted the seat next to him. Elise felt grateful at that moment she had worn pants, as she hoisted herself up and looked out to the sea. The golden sun illuminated the icy blue water, like a soft filter had been placed over the entire city region.

Luc continued. "I went to the mausoleum where he's buried. I thought I could be alone with him and try out the forgiveness you suggested. And guess who I found?" he asked, a wry smile forming on his lips. She was so close to him, she could smell the unmistakable scent of his aftershave.

"How did it go?" she asked, her mouth feeling dry. She licked her lips, wishing she had lip-gloss handy.

Luc shrugged and leaned back on his hands, as best he could on that small ledge. Joie pulled on her leash to eat the bread that had been thrown to the nearby pigeons, but that little dog paid no notice, instead scarfing down as much bread as she could.

"She was there mourning my father," he said, shaking his head, looking out to sea. "I couldn't believe it. I wouldn't have believed it, if I hadn't seen it with my two eyes. She goes there once a week, in any weather, to be with him." He turned to face her again. "I think she really loved him."

Elise was shocked. "Are you okay?"

Luc frowned, and she saw his jaw clench and unclench a few times before he spoke again. "I don't know. I guess. It's helped me figure out a few questions I never would have had answered. Which, probably would have taken me decades to figure out," he chuckled.

"Oh yeah?" Elise asked him.

Luc nodded. "Yeah. She really did. Love him, that is. She realized too late that she never really loved me. She had tears in her eyes. She was super apologetic about the mess and disarray she had created for our family," he said, his eyes glazing over. Elise watched him blink back tears. "I realized that this person I thought I loved never existed the way I thought. She was trapped within her own self and was never the one for me. She got caught up and then tried to be sincere when she realized that she couldn't live a life of lies. A huge weight was lifted when she said that, and I suppose a huge weight was lifted from her. The feeling of relief was very strong as we said our goodbyes."

Elise exhaled a sigh of relief. "So, what's next then?" she asked him, a smile forming on her face.

Luc shifted in his seat. "Well, I guess the next step for me is taking over Dubonier Enterprises."

Elise nodded. "Wow. Sounds like a big job."

Luc shrugged, biting his lip and looking out at the sea. "I guess. Hey..." he said, turning to her. "If I ever need someone to talk to–"

"—Don't worry," Elise jumped in. "I'll be there."

Chapter Eighteen

The next few days passed quickly. There was no more contact between them since Elise and Luc had spoken on the waterfront. She had wished him well at his new job. She expected that he was knee deep in work by this point and was not likely to call or text. Just in case, she had kept her phone close to her since their last meeting. Whenever her phone buzzed, she picked up but when she saw that she had gotten a text–from Rose, Rhonda, or Jacques or anyone else–she felt somewhat let down. Not that she would admit that to anyone and not that she hadn't on the surface been happy to hear from them.

Jacques was putting everything together to make their showing public. They had gotten a series of brochures made up–same homemade paper, fewer flowers–and had the photographer scheduled for later that day.

Meanwhile, she still hadn't heard back yet from the Dominiques regarding whether they wanted to bid on Luc's house. Elise cursed herself for not having been more thorough. I should have baked something more Provençal she told herself. Lavender meringues. Olive loaf. *Anything*.

Elise' phone buzzed. Jacques had texted her ten times already about details that were already decided so she didn't pick up too quickly. She had already prepared her response when she saw the caller's name come up: Luc Dubonier.

"*Bonjour* Monsieur Dubonier," she greeted him mock formally, the way she imagined he was addressed at work.

Luc groaned. "Not you too. No one here will call me Luc, no matter how many times I tell them," he said, laughing. "What's up?"

"Uh, not much, I'm fine," she said, looking around her mess of a hotel room which was scattered with brochures made of the homemade paper, and clothes she hadn't yet put away. "I'm heading to your house later to meet with the photographer. What's up? You called me," she realized. She laughed. Only Luc would call her and ask 'what's up'.

"Well, I've called about real estate," he said, his voice lowering to a whisper. "I need you to help me with a name transfer on a property of mine."

"Oh," Elise said, startled. She hadn't expected that. "Okay, no problem." She pulled out her laptop and dragged it onto her lap as she sat on her bed, opening up a new blank document to take notes. "Okay. Ready. What property?"

"The Dalmatian Estate," he replied, not missing a beat.

It took Elise a moment to clue in. "What do you..."

"I'm giving it to you," he said, pleased with himself from the sound of his voice. "I've got to get back to work–they don't give the boss a break," he said with a laugh. "If you could just get those documents drafted, we must get them to a lawyer to ensure there is no conflict of interest–"

"No," Elise said, cutting him off. "I'm sorry, but no. I can't take that house."

Luc exhaled in frustration. "Sure you can. It used to be yours, and now it will be yours again. It's as simple as you just taking it. There's no need to complicate it with–"

"—I'm not drafting anything!" she said.

"I bought it on a whim, so I can sell it on a whim." he said, laughing.

Elise scoffed. "A whim for you, perhaps. But this is much bigger than you're making it out to be!" she said, doing her best to contain her quivering voice.

"Seriously, just take it," he said again.

"Okay. How's this for an answer: No. I'm sure you have to get back to work, I'll go back to work. Let's just forget about this whole thing—"

"You're taking the house," he said, as if this was a game.

"Am not," she replied.

"Am, too."

"Am not!"

"Am, too!"

"Stop it! How old are you?" she laughed even though it annoyed her. This was serious.

"Okay, today you win."

He said goodbye and hung up. Elise didn't know what to think. Or how to feel. She had never been offered anything like this before. She doubted most people had. It was certainly not a problem she would be able to Google.

And more than anything, she wanted to know why her first instinct had been to say a resounding "no!"

Almost as soon as Elise had hung up the phone, it began to ring again. Why wasn't he listening to her? Why was he being like this? She picked up the phone.

"Seriously, I'm not taking the house," Elise began.

"Hello? Elise?" a woman's voice said from the other end of the line. Elise gulped and checked her screen. Clara.

"Hi, Clara, sorry! Mix up," she said in her most professional tones. "How is everything?"

Clara didn't seem fazed. "We've thought about it. We want the house. We'll pay the full asking price."

Elise barely knew what to say. She worked on autopilot. "Okay, fantastic," she said, doing her best to keep her tone normal. "I'll have the paperwork drafted and have a courier send it to you by tomorrow. Fantastic news."

After saying a flurry of goodbyes, she hung up the phone, feeling heat traveling up to her cheeks. A commission on eighty-eight million. *Eighty-eight million*. She felt dizzy and lay down on the bed to steady herself.

Elise didn't know what to do. She felt like she should scream. Calling Jacques and Luc seemed like the obvious thing to do. So why did she feel so frozen?

Chapter Nineteen

Celebrations ensued from Jacques' end the moment she called.

"No way!" he kept repeating. She could hear the cork popping off of the champagne bottle. "We've got to celebrate. Get over here! We are hitting the most fantastic restaurant to celebrate this afternoon."

Elise laughed. It was too bad that Clara hadn't called later that evening. She knew that it would be a halt-all-of-the-work kind of day for Jacques. "Okay. I'll call Luc and tell him to meet us."

Her whole body tensed as the phone rang. Unlike the last time she had tried to reach him urgently, he picked up on the second ring.

"We've got an offer!" she told him, before he even said hello. There was a stunned silence from the other end. "Hello?"

"Yeah, I'm here," she heard. Luc sounded as shocked as she felt. "I didn't think that would happen so quick. Especially, well, given the price..."

"Neither did I," she admitted. "But Clara just called me. I mean, nothing is final yet. Not until we have all the signatures in place. But Jacques is confident enough that he wants us to go celebrate with him meanwhile."

Luc's silence spoke volumes. Elise felt transported back to when her own family home was sold. She recalled how much she was relieved that she wouldn't be pummeled with memories at every waking moment. She had desperately needed that influx of cash to pay for the bank loans, taxes and immediate funeral costs. And, it was her house. Her home. Despite the memories, it was where she had become herself. She knew there was no clean or easy way of parting with something that sentimental. It pained her to even think of it. She thought back to the selfless offer Luc had made earlier, offering her the house. Was it her pride that was keeping her from taking it? She knew he could afford it.

Luc finally broke the silence. "Okay. Where should I meet you two?"

"Jacques' office. The Maison Leveque."

"I'll be there in half an hour."

Elise had gotten ready in record speed. Numbers kept flashing in her head. Eighty-eight million. Eighty-eight million. Every so often she would just let out a squeal of delight and think of everything she could buy with her money.

She could buy not one, but *two* yachts. She could buy back her old house–the Dalmatian Estate–for a fair price. She could pay off her mortgage on her condominium. She could travel the world. She could even buy a house in the South of France. The possibilities were endless. A thrill ran through her. She wouldn't need to work–she could just invest her money. She applied her lipstick carefully, albeit with a shaking hand, in the bathroom mirror. She examined her reflection carefully. She could have a lipstick custom made to suit her complexion.

She thought of Luc, and her excitement burst like a bubble. Luc loved that house. She knew he did. He was acting on a whim; just like he had been when he went away to travel for six months, not letting anyone really knows where he was. It was what he did when he bought that house in Ashfield. Elise certainly hadn't known Luc for long, but there was one thing she knew about him–he was impulsive.

Elise had applied her makeup and got dressed in a minimalist olive linen shift dress with floppy bows on the shoulders, her espadrilles, and Lord. She was feeling like that purse had been through everything with her–as much a part of Marseille for her as the people she had met.

She had to get to Maison Leveque as quickly as possible to make sure everything was perfect. She whipped out her phone and gave Mario a call.

"Hi Mario, I have to go to the office. I need you right away."

"Right away? Right away? It may be the right time for you, but maybe the wrong time for me. Maybe I'm just in the middle of painting the recreation on canvas of a pier on the old port. Ah, it is looking *merveilleuse*!"

"I'm so sorry, I will call a taxi."

"Madam! You will not. I will be there before you hang up your phone. I only wanted to let you know the tremendous sacrifice that I willingly make on your behalf."

"I truly appreciate all that you do. And there will be some celebrating there for you."

He was certainly the most helpful person she had met in Marseille. If he had driven an Uber, back in Ashfield, she imagined they would have created a special rating system for him–10 out of 5 stars. His familiar black car pulled up outside of the hotel within minutes.

"I was actually just eating at a restaurant around the corner. I finished the painting last night, and it is *magnifique*! " he said jovially, as she stepped in. "It must be fate that I am always available to serve you."

The pair of them traveled to the Maison Leveque. Along the way, Elise took the time to tell him everything. She hadn't talked to anyone about the house, the sale, and her conflicting feelings. As soon as she began, the words kept spilling out of her mouth until she had laid out the entire story from beginning to end, not having left a single stone unturned.

Mario, completely taken aback, shook his head in wonder. "*Mon dieu*. Well, it sounds like you don't want him to sell it," he said plainly.

Elise was surprised. Surely that's not what she had said. "I just mean, I'm excited for the commission. But..."

Mario jumped in. "Let me tell you something, Elise," he began, looking far more at her than he was at the traffic. Elise, although interested in what he had to say, wished he just kept his eyes on the road a little more. "I have lived in a lot of places in the world. Marseille for the longest. And if anyone I have ever met in my travels was offered the commission you have been, on that kind of sale..." he let out a low whistle. "... let me tell you. They would not be hesitating. Not for a single second."

When they arrived at the Maison Leveque, Elise insisted that he come in to celebrate. "Come on. You know the whole story. And it will be fun! Just, leave your keys at the office, perhaps, we will all need to take a taxi home." she said as an afterthought. She had never celebrated with Jacques or Mario before. If she was guessing correctly, neither of them would be upright by the end of the evening. It didn't take much convincing to get Mario to join her. As soon as she stepped into the office, celebrations were already underway.

"We did it!" Jacques called out, the second she stepped in. He had already pulled out a bottle of champagne. The sign on the door had already been turned around to say it was closed for the day. It was only noon. "*Felicitations*!"

Elise joined him by matching his enthusiasm and quickly introducing him to Mario. "The more the merrier," Jacques exclaimed, before pouring Mario a generous glass of champagne. The two of them hit it off immediately.

She kept looking from her phone to the window, waiting for Luc to arrive.

"Elise," Jacques called over to her. "You didn't tell me Mario was an artist! He's just shown me his artwork. I have to use it at my next open house for staging," he said excitedly. "Clients will love work from a local artist."

Mario looked thoroughly chuffed, as he continued showing Jacques his artwork on his phone. The clock continued ticking. Elise expected Luc to show up late. Perhaps not even at all. But he was right on time.

Luc's face broke into a genuine smile upon seeing her. All of her tension melted as soon as he began walking towards her. "So, it seems like my instincts about you were right," he said.

Elise felt her heart flutter in her chest. "What do you mean?"

Luc raised his eyebrows approvingly. "I mean, you sold my house. And in record time," he added.

Elise laughed. "Remember that it's not sold *yet*. We still have to go over all the details. Signing, signatures, that stuff."

"So, are you joining us in celebration?" Jacques asked, holding up a glass.

Luc threw his keys into a jar on the table. "I couldn't think of anything better."

The party was destined not to remain in the confines of an office. It was an hour later that the four of them were sitting at a restaurant in the Old Port, enjoying another bottle of champagne, and having ordered oysters, oysters, and more oysters. It was a decadent celebration. Elise was doing her best to enjoy every minute.

She couldn't help the rising feeling in her chest whenever she thought of another family living in that estate. What about Marliane? Where would she go? What about Luc, where would he live?

Elise knew that Luc would find a house, no problem. But would be find himself a *home*?

Jacques and Mario began arguing about the proper way to shuck an oyster. As Elise hadn't even known there was a proper way to shuck an oyster, she left them to their own merriment. She turned to appraise Luc, whose glazed over eyes and expression made her think perhaps this was perhaps a fantastic time to tell him what she really thought.

Then again, it could have been the champagne talking.

Just as Luc turned to her, about to say something, an uncontrollable urge overcame her as she sputtered out what she had thought she could control. "Luc, I don't know if I agree with the sale," she said, shocking herself as the words escaped.

She looked at him with eyes as wide as saucers, waiting for his reaction. But in typical Luc-fashion, he appeared unfazed. "You think I should ask for more?"

Elise laughed at the misunderstanding and gently shook her head. She was grateful that Mario and Jacques across from them were enthralled in another conversation and didn't appear to be listening.

"No, no you're not understanding what I'm trying to say," she persisted. Her words sounded a little slurred together, she noticed. She took a deep breath and steadied herself on her chair. "I think you should wait a little while before selling. You've only just arrived back in Marseille. What was it, a month ago? Don't you think you should wait a bit, to see how you feel in, I don't know... six months? A year? It's kind of a major decision," she said, doing her best to keep her words crisp and clear. "I mean, I know that things in the last year sucked, to put it lightly, but your grandfather built that house. It's a symbol of your family. Don't you want to preserve that, at least?"

Luc sat there in steely silence. She wondered if she had gone too far. If she had pushed the wrong button. "You think I should hold on to it?" he finally asked. Elise shot a quick glance to Jacques and Mario to see if they were listening, but their conversation had turned even more heated, as they now involved a passing waiter, garnering his input.

Elise turned back to Luc. "Yeah, I think you should. At least wait. You don't have to keep making these bold, fast decisions," she said. "You don't have to keep uprooting. Sometimes, it's nice to stay put. Even in tough times."

She mentally revised all the times she had told herself she would escape Ashfield right after her parents had died. That constant feeling of having needing to get out. The memories had been too much. But for whatever reason, she had stuck it out. She still thought she was a better person for it. The connections she made, the friendships that had endured through the hardship–it had worked for her. And she thought even if that specifically didn't suit Luc, well, he was acting far too hastily.

He turned to her, an incredulous look on his face. "You are really willing to push off the sale, a commission that big, because you think it would be better for me *emotionally*?"

Elise nodded. "Look Luc. Do what's best for you. Anger aside, hurt aside, pain aside–just think about it." Her heart was pounding at her boldness. As the words had spilled out of her, she knew that they were true.

Her phone rang, and Elise checked the number. Rose. It must have been midnight back in Ashfield. She held up a finger to Luc and stood up, walking away from the table. She picked up as soon as she was out of earshot from the rest of the table.

"Hey, what's up?" she asked. There was a lot of noise in the background wherever Rose was calling from.

"Hey, don't panic," Rose started. Just hearing those two words–*don't panic*–made her do just the opposite. Her mind flashed to the worst-case scenarios.

"What's wrong?" she demanded.

Rose exhaled dramatically. "You said you weren't going to panic!"

"Rose!" Elise nearly wailed. "Just tell me what happened."

"Okay. There was a fire," Rose told her.

Elise's mind felt like a ping-pong ball, hitting every worst-case situation. "A fire?" she echoed. "Where?"

"At the condo. But don't worry, no one was hurt," Rose said. "And Langdon and I got out okay."

Elise's head felt like it was spinning in circles. "You're not serious," she demanded. Even though Rose liked to joke, she would never take it this far.

"And, our condo? Is it okay?" Elise asked, her voice rising by at least an octave. She didn't even want to know. "It was the thermostat, wasn't it?"

"It wasn't the thermostat. But they haven't let anyone back in."

"Do they know where the fire started?"

Rose was quick to respond on that one. "They think it started in one of the recreational rooms. My guess is maybe the microwave. Something like that. I dunno. The fire department is still investigating," she said.

The two of them remained silent for a couple of moments. "Well, I'm just glad you two are safe. Along with everyone else," she mustered the energy to say.

"Yeah, me too. Sorry to call with such bad news on your vacation. Working vacation, I mean," she said.

"Where are you now? Where are you going to stay?" Elise suddenly asked, feeling urgent. The sounds of fire sirens blared in the distant background.

"With Rhonda," Rose declared, and Elise instantly felt herself relax. "The thing is, they need all of this insurance information from you. But I don't know where any of it is."

Elise did her best to remain level-headed. "I'll be back in Ashfield as soon as I can. Not long," she promised.

"Okay," Rose said. "I miss you, sis."

Elise swallowed the lump in her throat, tears pricking her eyes. "I'll see you soon." She walked back to the table where the trio of men didn't seem to notice her puffy eyes.

"Elise! How do you eat lobster?" Jacques immediately demanded, while Mario shook his head in the background. "Butter or no butter?"

"She is American!" Mario protested. "She likes it with butter. I'm right, right?" he asked, looking to her for confirmation.

It was true, but Elise wasn't about to get caught up in their escapades. "I think I'm just going to get my share of the bill," she said finally. "I'm pretty wiped."

Jacques and Mario bid their farewells, continuing to enjoy every moment of their heated debate. When she finally paid, they had moved onto debating the best bread in the city.

"The proper way to cut a baguette..." was the last thing she heard, as she stood up to leave. As she turned, she caught Luc's eye. He gave her a tight, closed-lips smile and nodded in her direction. She returned the smile before taking off. It was done. The house was being sold. Eighty-eight million. Eighty-eight million. She'd repeated that number so many times to herself but now she was feeling more and more distant from what it meant. It began ringing hollow in her head, a vague sound in an empty room. She wasn't sure if she was just exhausted, or perhaps it was all the champagne, but she felt less of a thrill thinking about that commission check as she walked along the water's edge.

Chapter Twenty

The following day, Elise woke up to a flurry of text messages from Jacques.

Have you talked to Luc?

What happened?

Did he say anything to you?

Call me when you get this

Elise looked down at the messages in surprise. Almost as soon as she had looked at the messages she received a call from the concierge on her room phone.

"*Madame*, there is a Monsieur Luc Dubonier here to see you."

Elise's heart thudded in her chest. What was Luc doing? What had happened?

A flurry of thoughts raced through her mind as she threw on a black jumpsuit and mules, tossing her hair into a high bun. At the last minute, and she added a touch of lip-gloss, before she ran to the elevator. It felt like an eternity, as the elevator seemed to stop at every floor on the way down.

As soon as the elevator doors opened, Elise immediately locked eyes with Luc, waiting in the lobby. But his appearance just the opposite of what she had expected. His beard was groomed, his hair combed, and his shirt looked like it had been ironed. When he saw her, his face broke into a nervous grin.

"Hey," he said, his eyes looking alert as he walked towards her. "I have something to tell you." As he got closer, he grabbed her hand and led her to a nearby sofa in a quiet corner of the lobby. "Thank you," he said urgently, his eyes shining. What was going on?

Elise raised her eyebrows. "Thank you?" she repeated, as he nodded.

"After our talk yesterday, well, I had some thinking to do," he admitted. "I called up Annette. We ended up talking for hours." Luc's expression suddenly became animated, as he smiled from ear to ear. She had never seen him looking so *happy*. "You know what, she doesn't think I should sell the house either. And she has a lot to gain from the sale, too," he added.

"Wow, that's amazing–" Elise faltered.

"This morning," Luc continued. "I had a chat with Marliane. You were right," he declared, shaking his head incredulously. "I shouldn't sell the house. I knew it deep down. It was why I came in to check on those two people who wanted to buy it. I don't want them living there. It is why I priced it so high, I think. You know, Jacques had warned me against pricing it that high to begin with, but I wouldn't listen to him. I listened to you though."

Elise felt like she had been slapped. Luc sat beside her, beaming with pride. He had her to thank? Had she been that persuasive? A warm feeling arose in her chest, which she instantly did her best to quell.

"Luc, are you sure?"

He continued, this time more slowly. "I feel like I never gave this house a chance to be a home. No one did. Not my grandfather, or my father. I'd like to make a go of it."

It took Elise a moment to register what he was really saying. She had remembered Luc having talked about his grandfather's determination. Surely, he hadn't spent enough time in that house to enjoy it. His father, well, from what she had put together from the bits and pieces Luc had said, it sounded like he had never been home too. No one who really made that house home. Even now.

He would not sell the house. And it was all because of her.

"Are you feeling all right?" she finally asked tentatively.

Luc laughed softly, a look of quiet determination overcoming him. "Honestly, I haven't felt this good in a long time." He seemed to have grown up overnight. As if the weight of the decision, and finally stopping the trail of faulty decisions he had made, was being dropped.

"Well, I know as your realtor, I should be disappointed. But as your, uh, friend," Elise said, pausing at her use of the word *friend*. Was that all that they were? She cleared her throat. "As your friend, I think you're making the right decision. Grief makes you do crazy things. It makes you act before you think. I just, I just wouldn't want you to ever regret selling your home."

"No, you don't get it," he said while shaking his head straightaway, as if trying to collect his thoughts. "*You* made it home."

Elise felt winded, as she repeated his words in her mind. She had made the Marseille mansion a home?

Luc cleared his throat and continued. "I mean it was a home. But I mean, it became so clear what was missing when you arrived." Elise felt like she was spinning. "Your touches. Your presence," he said, reaching out to take her hand. She gently squeezed his hand, sending a shooting electric feeling throughout her body.

Elise's throat tightened. She could barely get the words out. "Wow, Luc, I don't know what to say," was all she responded. Her heart was going a mile a minute, and her cheeks already felt hot. This certainly hadn't been what she was expecting. As she examined him, she saw a swell of pride about him. "I mean, I think you're making the right decision," she said, after careful consideration. It was true. She thought he was making the right decision.

Luc nodded, squeezing her hand once more. "I know."

"I just want you to do well. To be happy," she continued.

He smiled. "I know you do. It seemed like you were the only one, for a while there," he said with a soft laugh. "I just feel horrible you've come out all of this way. With no commission cheque. No sale."

Now it was Elise's turn to laugh. "Don't worry. It's been worth it. It's funny–I feel like talking to you about everything has helped me heal too. I never really took that time that I needed to properly grieve. I definitely buried myself in work, and well, I don't think it was always the right decision," she admitted.

"You can't heal what you don't feel, right?" Luc said, and Elise laughed.

"Maybe hire a consultant. Or ask Marliane for help. She's capable of so much, you know," Elise began. "I can imagine it's all a lot," she whispered.

Luc nodded. "You might be right."

"And maybe watch out for what girls you go for," she said, lightly teasing him. This was a question burning up inside of her, but she was too afraid to ask.

He smiled. "I think you're right about that too. But I don't think you're too much trouble," he said teasingly.

Elise suddenly realized just how close the two of them were sitting. Slowly, he began to lean towards her. Her heart began thumping. He was going to kiss her.

"*Madame* Laird? *Monsieur* Dubonier?" they heard suddenly in a rapt voice, making Elise jump as Luc pulled away. A tall man wearing the hotel staff uniform spoke to them. "You have a visitor."

From across the lobby, Elise watched as Jacques made his way across the marble floor. From the looks of things, he was fuming.

"I'll be back in a moment. Don't move a muscle," Luc said, flashing her a grin. As he stood up and spoke to Jacques, who from the looks of things, didn't seem to be taking Luc's change of heart as well as she had.

Elise drew a deep breath. What was she doing? She barely had time to collect her thoughts. To figure things out. The last thing Luc needed right now was more complications. More difficulty. He had just started to get things figured out. How on earth was getting involved with her going to help matters, especially considering that she was about to go back to Ashfield. As Luc returned, content at having pacified Jacques, who was now quietly waiting by the front desk.

"I promised him lunch at the restaurant here, the same one we went to," he said, his eyes flashing and making her stomach doing that swooping-thing he seemed so good at. "Seems he's a sucker for Michelin stars too," he teased.

As he walked closer to her, returning to his seat, Elise gathered the confidence to speak. "The last thing you need right now is more complication. I'm getting on a plane to go back to Ashfield tonight." As she said it out loud, she knew she would book the flight right away. "There's been a fire at home, and I need to get back there."

Luc looked surprised. "A fire?" He suddenly went white as a sheet. "It wasn't the thermostat, was it?"

Elise couldn't help but let a giggle escape. "No, it wasn't the thermostat."

He looked relieved momentarily. "If it had been, I would have to have made sure you took the house on Dalmatian Street," he said, before getting revved up again. "But in all seriousness, is everyone okay? Is your place damaged?"

Elise nodded. "Yes, everyone is okay. And yes to the second question too. I don't really know where we will live for now. But that's not the point," she said, shaking her head and trying not to let herself get too emotional about it all. "The point is, your home is Marseille. My home is Ashfield. This–" she said, pointing back and forth between the two of them. "—would make things complicated. And the very last thing you need right now is complicated. You've had more than a lifetime's worth of complications in the last year."

Before Luc could say anything, Elise stood up and walked back to the elevator, careful that the doors shut before she burst into tears.

Chapter Twenty-One

Within one day, Elise's bags were packed. Joe had booked her flight back to Ashfield. And her checkout from the hotel was only a few hours away. Although her heart skipped a beat anytime her phone buzzed, she had been disappointed to see it wasn't Luc.

Then again, she had been the one who rejected him. When her phone buzzed this time, it was from Mario.

Meet at Le Pharo in one hour?

Elise shot back a text as quick as lightning. Her thoughts felt scattered. Her mind was going a mile a minute. Ever since she had decided to leave–or as Joe had so sensitively put it, 'since she had gotten the boot from the job'- she felt hopelessly disoriented. But she had stuck to distracting herself as best she could, packing, unpacking, and then repacking her belongings.

When the word got out that the sale of the Marseille mansion was off, Elise's phone had blown up. Mario and Jacques insisted on a goodbye party, but after they had heard just how quickly her flight had been booked, had planned a picnic in the courtyard of Le Pharo. It was the building that had led to her near-success. She expected that long after she was gone, Mario and Jacques' friendship would endure. Jacques had taken to using his art in the houses he staged, and Mario always seemed to have something better–something even more opulent–for show. Even when the house didn't sell, the browsers of the homes had typically inquired about the art. And Jacques, being the sales-man he was, had offered to broker the sales–with a commission.

Elise made her way to Le Pharo, for what she expected would be her last time, all the while taking in how the golden light shimmered against the light blue sea. Memorizing the pastel hues, the snippets of rapid-fire French she heard from passer-by's, and the cavalcade of sailboats in the harbor. As she walked along the shoreline, a familiar face came into view. How did she know him?

"Santi?" she heard herself call out, as if someone else was operating her voice.

He turned to look at her, and she suddenly realized that he was holding hands with someone. Someone *beautiful* with long dark hair and a minuscule waist. Someone who *didn't* look as happy as she felt to see a familiar face. Recognition dawned on Santi's face within moments.

"Ah, Liz, was it?" he asked with the same warm and friendliness she had remembered.

"Elise," she said. "Hi, I met Santi on one of his tours," she said to the woman, who up close was even more beautiful and intimidating. But as soon as she said that, the woman's face softened.

"People love his tours," she said, giving Santi an affectionate poke in the arm.

"Was it you who I gave that awful love advice?" Santi asked, scrunching up his face to remember. "I think whoever it was, I felt terrible about that."

Elise laughed. "Yeah. It was me."

"Well, I'm happy I–or I should say *we*–ran into you," he said, giving his girlfriend an excited smile. "I was head over heels in love. And heart broken. I realized as soon as I gave that awful lecture about love how wrong I was. I called up Lisette as soon as that tour was done."

Lisette was radiant, and Elise noticed on her finger–a very important one–a thin gold band with a sparkling ring, subtly reflecting the sun. If she had known them better, she would have given them both hugs. But she thought better of it.

"I couldn't be happier for you," she gushed. As they said their goodbyes, and she continued on her way, she couldn't help but think back to what she had learned on that tour with Santi. Marseille–a city of loss and rebirth. She wondered how long it would be before she found love herself. And if that love had any bearings in Marseille.

As much as she loved Ashfield, it tugged at her heartstrings to leave. As she drew nearer to the seaside manor Le Pharo, it became clear that she was in for more than she had bargained for. Picnics back in Ashfield were usually composed of a few chicken salad sandwiches and watermelon slices. Nothing more. But this...

A red and white checked blanket had been laid out. There was a wooden cutting board that had been set out, with a variety of cheeses still wrapped. Two baguettes were strewn across the blanket. A small cooler with wine peaking out made her heart skip a beat. Mario and Jacques were too busy, deep in conversation, to notice as she walked up.

"Am I interrupting anything?" she asked, breaking into a broad grin. Mario leaped to his feet and immediately enveloped her into a hug–American-style.

"Elise, we will miss you," he said, holding her shoulders and looking at her solemnly. "You are certain there is no way for you to stay?"

Before him, Jacques had popped the cork on a bottle of champagne. He gave her a sad smile as he handed her a glass.

"I second Mario," Jacques agreed, pushing his friend out of the way to give her a kiss on each cheek. Emotions willed up inside her she hadn't intended to feel. This was a happy lunch. A celebration of sorts. She did her best to fight the tears threatening to escape.

"I wish I could stay," she said, taking a sip of the champagne appreciatively. It was *parfait*—chilled, semi dry, with notes of honey. She sat down on the blanket, fetching her sunglasses out of Lord as the bright light nearly blinded her. "I can't thank you both enough. You've made me feel so at home here."

Mario and Jacques exchanged a knowing glance. "You know," Jacques began. "You seem so at home here. Mario had even floated the idea–"

"—You should stay!" Mario blurted out, as Jacques looked to him with disdain. "I mean," Mario said, this time more carefully. "You could work at Maison Leveque. With Jacques. Or maybe take over as a driver for my business."

Elise's eyebrows shot up. "Why? Where are you going?"

Mario looked pleased and Jacques puffed up. "Well, my clients love Mario's work. Enough so that Mario now seems to have enough work to keep him busy full time. *More* than full-time."

Mario shook his head good-naturedly. "No, I'm not going to kill myself working to the bone for your clients," he said teasingly. "But it is true. Now, I need to hire another person to be a driver for my old business. It is tiring work, being so successful," he said with a shrug. "Any chance you want to be a driver?"

Elise laughed. The two of them would make a good team, she knew. Mario wouldn't be fazed by Jacques demands, and she knew that Mario would more than deliver on his promises. There was a part of her that yearned to stay. She wanted to join the team. She wanted to spend more time on the Old Port, drinking wine with Jacques and Mario. She wanted to get to know Marseille even better. And most of all, she wanted to stay for one person in particular.

She wished that she could. If she were younger, perhaps. If she didn't have Rose, she could consider it. If that job offer to be a partner at Cotherington Realty hadn't been that tempting...

"Thank you," she said, looking from Mario's expectant face to Jacques'. She really was. "But I'm afraid today, I'll be saying *bon voyage* to you both. And..." she added with sadness creeping into her voice. "...to Marseille."

Chapter Twenty-Two

When Elise arrived back in Ashfield, she felt like she had been gone much longer than a week.

"Welcome home!" Joe said, when he met her at the airport. "Or should I say, *Bienvenue*!"

Elise laughed, giving her boss a hug. "It's good to see you. I'm sorry about the sale," she said, pulling a face. She had called Joe from the airport in Marseille earlier, letting him know that she had switched her flight.

"Nonsense," he said in that way of his that made everything feel all right. "It's just good to have you home."

Joe helped Elise carry her bags to his Volvo station wagon, which was filled with golfing equipment in the back. "We'll have to put your luggage in the backseat. Golf bags take up a lot of room." he said with a laugh, and him and Elise crammed her enormous suitcases into the backseat. He had been slipping into his semi-retirement nicely. She sat up front, as he turned on the radio. "Mind if we make a quick stop at the office before I drop you off at home? Or where is it you're staying anyway?" he asked, suddenly looking at her with concern. He had heard about the fire in her condominium, it seemed. She was certain it was the buzz all over Ashfield.

"Rose, Langdon, and I are at Rhonda's for a few nights, just until everything clears up," she told him. Joe knew Rhonda–she had worked as a receptionist one summer while completing her master's degree. She was the best receptionist they had ever had, Joe had said repeatedly, and even offered Rhonda a wildly ridiculous pay-raise at the end of the summer, enticing her to stay. Elise always suspected that Rhonda's passion for psychology had translated into her being the office-therapist that summer, but she had never asked.

"Humph," he grunted. "Langdon will not be too happy about that," he said, referring to the fact that Rhonda too had cats. Elise marveled at Joe's light-hearted exterior, while capable of remembering the smallest of facts about other people.

Elise stifled a yawn. "Yeah, sure. No problem." She never had mastered sleeping on airplanes and was thoroughly exhausted by the time that Joe pulled up outside of Cotherington Realty. It felt strange somehow, being back in Ashfield after her time in Marseille. As Joe parked and opened up his door, she breathed in the familiar salty air and sweet grass scent that permeated Ashfield in the late summer.

"Why don't you come on in with me?" he suggested. Elise didn't see the point, but did as he requested anyway–partially out of habit, and partially out of the lack of energy she had to question him. As soon as she walked in through the glass and chrome double doors, she nearly fell backwards in shock.

"Surprise!" the entire team at Cotherington Realty screamed in delight, as she walked in. She looked to Joe, who had a happy and guilty expression on his face.

Elise broke into a grin. "What's all this?" she asked, turning to take in every co-worker who had come in to celebrate. She looked at the cake, which she now saw had writing on the top.

Happy Birthday and Promotion Elise! it said.

She shook her head in delight. "You guys!"

Joe clapped her on the back. "Now, after we're finished this cake, how about getting us more million-dollar sales?" he said with a chuckle.

Elise laughed, tried hard not to think of the big one that got away across the Atlantic, and gratefully accepted the large slice of cake handed to her. "No problem," she said breezily, and took a big delicious bite.

The surprises that day didn't stop. Elise met with Rose later that day at Frakas and was presented with an envelope.

"Open it," Rose said eagerly, barely able to conceal her excitement as she squirmed in her seat across from her.

Elise eyed her sister cautiously as she opened up the envelope. Inside was a cheque, for twenty thousand dollars. Her brow furrowed as her heart sunk. "Where did you get this money?" she asked.

But Rose's smile grew. "I made it."

"Made it? How?" Elise asked cautiously. Her heart fluttered in anxious trepidation. Surely, Rose hadn't taken out a loan to pay her back? She couldn't imagine a worst-case scenario.

But Rose shook her head, as if reading her thoughts. "You don't have to worry. I made it. It's mine. *Legally*," she insisted.

Elise's eyes narrowed. "But you were fired. And surely they weren't paying you this well, or else I'm sure you wouldn't have been fired." She pulled a face. "No offence."

Rose laughed and held up her hands like she was being held at gunpoint. "None taken." Her sister took a deep breath, and she looked to be collecting herself for what she said next. "I started selling my vintage finds on Instagram for a profit!" she finally exclaimed in a rapid-fire sentence. Rose looked relieved and thrilled to have told her, like a shaken up champagne bottle with the cork finally popped.

It took Elise a moment to register what her sister was saying. "So, you mean to tell me that you have been selling vintage items of clothing–"

"—and accessories," Rose interrupted.

"Okay. So Clothing and accessories. You're selling them on Instagram? What happened with the liquidator?"

"He turned out to be a fraud. He wanted to give me a cheque for ten thousand and I said he would have to go to the bank with me to get it certified. On the way to the bank, he disappeared."

Elise was impressed at her sister's business savvy–even *she* might have gotten caught in that trap. It was clear Rose had learned a thing or two while she was gone.

"So what happened next?"

"I was frustrated and went for a drive out of town. I stopped at a lawn sale where I noticed some superb items being sold for practically nothing. I bought them and then posted pictures of me on Instagram advertising them. It all linked to my new website..." she said, pulling out her phone and thrusting it at Elise to examine. She had to admit, it looked fantastic. "I thought, I could take pictures of some items in the inventory and sell them on-line."

Elise didn't know what to say and shook her head in admiration. "Seriously, I'm impressed," she admitted.

Rose's smile grew by the minute. "Remember how mom was into purses?"

Elise's heart sunk. "Rose, you didn't."

Luckily, her sister pulled a face. "Obviously I didn't sell mom's purses. I'm not a psycho. Who do you think I am?" Elise breathed a sigh of relief before

Rose continued. "No. Mom taught me what quality was. To have a good eye for stuff. So I did it four more times last week. I've been driving all over the state, looking for luxury items that are being sold at undervalued prices, restoring them with a little of leather polish and sometimes fixing up a zipper or button, and then re-selling them, mostly using my Instagram account for advertising, and I'm getting paid what they are worth!" Rose said with pride. "Which is a lot," she added as an afterthought.

Elise couldn't help but laugh. "Well, you're certainly putting your skills to work."

"Plus, I've got a schedule of places to visit this week coming up, and the inventory has been reduced by a bit. I'll only keep buying what I can afford from the money I've made. It turns out you don't need an actual shop to make money."

Elise shook her head. She should never have doubted Rose's ingenuity. She had just needed to find her way. And she would be reluctant to tell Rhonda that yet again, she had been right.

"Wow. I don't really know what to say," she replied. "I mean, I am just so happy for you."

Just then, Mary popped over with a plate piled high with fresh tomatoes, feta, and greens. "You should be proud of this girl–or should I say, young woman!" Mary said, grabbing Rose by the cheek and beaming with pride. "She's been running all over town–no–the State. And mind you, it's been worthwhile," she hinted. "I am now the proud owner of Louis," she said, dawning her new Speedy handbag. "Beautiful, no?"

Elise couldn't help but smile. This community, her family and extended family, they were all in it together.

A week passed by uneventfully. Elise had some nice houses to show, and nice people who seemed interested in buying them. She had talked with the insurance company and camped out at Rhonda's house in the suburbs. Apparently, the entire condo building was quite damaged. Although it was mostly smoke, electrical and water damage. The future of that building was unknown–the rebuilding and repairs yet to begin. Meanwhile, their belongings had been into storage. Elise had double-checked that the storage unit was fireproof, just in case.

"Seriously, we will get all of this sorted soon, and get out of your hair," Elise had said to Rhonda every morning since they had arrived, while she made pancakes to make their presence less of a disturbance. But Rhonda shook her head each time.

Langdon had already made himself quite at home, snuggled into the corner of the breakfast nook in the kitchen. Joe had been wrong. It turned out that Langdon had taken a shining to Rhonda's cat named Fish. Fish hopped up to snuggle with Langdon and the two of them purred in unison.

"It seems like love is in the air," Rhonda remarked, looking in their direction.

"He'll be devastated when we go back home. Maybe we can have cat playdates," she teased, but as the words came out of her mouth, thought might be a good idea.

"You are welcome as long as you like!" Rhonda insisted each time Elise mentioned leaving.

Despite Rhonda's persistent telling her otherwise, Elise felt that she was overstepping. Since having returned, Elise learned that after more back and forth over email, Howard had declared his love for Rhonda in front of the entire country club, which in turn had erupted into thunderous applause. Well, considering the venue, perhaps not *thunderous*. But it had been enough for Rhonda, who now no longer felt like she was the other woman involved in a clandestine affair. She had proudly gotten back from driving Howard's three sons to soccer practice that morning, all before Elise had even woken up.

That day, the trio sat in the breakfast nook of Rhonda's spacious kitchen, overlooking the Ashfield Golf and Country Club. Elise had shown the property to Rhonda and her then-husband years earlier. Rhonda had kept it in the divorce, and Elise was grateful. It was a stunning home, on just over an acre of land, in a quiet resort-style neighborhood.

"So, now that you finally have a day off, why don't you go spend a bit of time on the golf course?" Rhonda suggested to Elise, and she took a bite of the fluffy pancakes she had made. Elise took a moment to assess her options. She could spend the afternoon golfing. Rose was off doing some mystery errand, and Rhonda was taking off shortly to meet with her mother in town. It would be the first time she introduced her to Howard, and her nervousness showed.

"You could always join us, if you're in the mood for the symphony," Rhonda said pleadingly.

Elise knew that three was a crowd, and four was definitely too many–especially when it came to symphonies. "Not really my cup of tea. But everything will go smoothly," she reassured her friend. "I have a good feeling about things. Besides, my horoscope said that love was on the horizon. It didn't say specially for me, so I'm assuming it is translating to the people *around* me."

Rhonda laughed. "I don't think horoscopes work like that," she teased, but already Rhonda looked visibly less worried.

"You know, I might head over to the swimming pool at the country club. I haven't been swimming in ages. It'll feel good to get some exercise," she said, thinking back to her calendar. She typically had days where she exercised marked with a red X. So far, for the months June and July, there were no X's in sight. And now it was nearly August.

"You sure I can't tempt you?" Rhonda asked in one last attempt. "They've taken out the intermission for the matinee show and are bringing in a quartet from Germany!"

Of all of their shared interests and hobbies, Elise still couldn't understand Rhonda's love of a symphony orchestra. "That is all you," she said, laughing. "I'll catch up with you later. Give my love to your mom and to Howard!" she said, clearing away the breakfast dishes, putting them in the dishwasher, and giving Langdon a pat on the head.

The swimming pool at the Ashfield Golf and Country Club was only a short walk away. Some residents on Rhonda's street preferred to use a golf cart to get around, but Elise made the journey on foot. After she arrived, signed in, and got changed in the clubhouse change room, she made her way to the pool. No sooner had she stepped foot out of the change room before she heard a familiar voice.

"Elise!" She craned her neck to see, in the bright sunlight, Gerard Remieux walking up to her. "How wonderful to see you," he said.

She gave him a kiss on each cheek and he looked bemused. "Wonderful to see you too," she agreed.

"Now, how did you like Marseille?" he asked, a twinkle in his eye. "You have not been back long, no?"

Elise shook her head. "No. I haven't been back for long. Just a month or so. It seems like it's flown by though," she said. Just thinking her whirlwind adventure had occurred a full month ago felt surprising.

"And you liked it?" he asked, eyebrows raised.

Elise smiled. "Loved it."

Gerard beamed at her. "Good, good. I heard my Godson stayed in the house though," he said in a curious tone. "*Tsk tsk*, bringing you out all that way. But I have to admit, he seems happy."

Elise felt a pang in her chest. It was the first she had heard of Luc since she had gotten home. She had checked her email and text messages almost every fifteen minutes after she had arrived back in Ashfield, convinced that he would have tried to reach out. But then again, it was *her* who had told him that it wouldn't work.

She drew a deep breath. "I'm glad to hear he's doing well."

Gerard shook his head. "Not well. Amazing!" He smiled a mega-watt smile, clasping his hands together. He leaned in and whispered to her. "Apparently, he has re-designed the company. He's been modernizing it, bringing it up to speed. He has been doing, well, very good. And he seems it," he said, tapping his head with his finger.

Elise laughed, feeling at once happy and sad. "I'm so glad to hear it," she said.

"And I heard you made quite the impression over there," Gerard began. "Don't write off Marseille just yet," he said, a twinkle in his eye. "I know it is not Ashfield, but it has its charm."

Elise was about to jump in to protest, to tell him she loved Marseille. But he continued on.

"Well, I must go," he said, a very tanned, scantily clad woman appearing by his side almost instantaneously. This time, the woman gave Elise a warm smile which Elise returned in spades.

"I'll see you soon," she said, bidding them both a good afternoon, before she dove into the pool to hopefully drown her discomfort.

Chapter Twenty-Three

Elise and Rose walked along the pier, watching the same crisp-white polo-wearing sailing crew take their sailboats out to sea. Another month had passed. Now that it was nearing the end of the season, those days were limited.

"Let's go this way," Rose insisted, while Elise pointed them towards the Port Roastery.

"Come on, I seriously need another cup of coffee," Elise said. Although it was only three in the afternoon, she had skipped her second cup that morning, and felt eerily on the verge of falling asleep mid-step.

Rose huffed. "Elise, there's this boat over there that I really want to check out," she said, pointing towards a row of yachts docked in the marina. "It might leave soon. Come on. Please?"

Elise rolled her eyes good-naturedly. "Fine. But after we're done looking at that boat, we're heading to get coffee," she said, to which Rose agreed.

As they walked on the pathway alongside the marina, Rose kept checking her phone.

"What, are you waiting for someone to call you?" Elise asked. "Did you meet someone?"

Rose kept her eyes resolute on the water, scanning the horizon. "I'm just looking for this specific one..." she murmured. Elise followed her gaze, where a series of boats were floating in the late summer bay.

"What on earth are you looking for?" Elise persisted. She felt acutely aware that they were walking further away from the Port Roastery with each step. "And since when have you been into boats?"

Rose didn't answer. She came to a full stop beside an empty mooring. Finally, Rose broke her silence. "There! Over there!" She pointed eagerly at a giant yacht which had just begun its journey into the harbor.

Elise had to admit, it was a nice boat. Crisp white, with gleaming chrome hardware that reflected the bright sunlight. And was that a flag for France it had attached? She did a double take, turning to look at Rose, who could barely contain her smile.

"Rose, what's going on?" she asked, putting her hand on her hip.

Rose shifted back and forth on her feet, before pointing to the boat. "Look!"

Elise saw as a figure from the front of the boat was waving in their direction. Rose waved in return. Elise wasn't sure if she should wave or not until she saw the specific outline of the figure.

"Elise, are you okay? You're white as a sheet," Rose said, putting a protective arm around her to steady her. The two-story yacht was getting closer and closer. Young men and women in chinos and boat shoes who worked at the marina helped to secure the yacht as it docked in the Ashfield harbor. And now that it was close up, there was no mistaking the identity of the man on board the ship.

"Luc?" Elise called out, as he ran across to the lower story of the boat and took a leap of faith onto the dock.

"Careful!" the crewman yelled at him, as Luc confidently strolled in their direction. Elise felt like her legs had turned into silly putty.

"What are you doing here?" she breathlessly asked him. He was drawing closer. He looked more tanned than when she had last seen him. No more dark circles under his eyes. He looked well rested. His hair was still disheveled, but this time she expected it was the wind. She turned to Rose. "Did you do this?" she sputtered.

Rose winked in her direction. "You're not the only one who can track down family, you know," she said with a laugh. "Annette says hi, by the way."

He broke into a wide smile upon seeing her, his eyes locked to hers.

"What are you doing here?" she asked him.

Luc stopped, just inches away from her. She could see the rise and fall of his chest as he took quick, shallow breaths. He was clearly nervous too.

"I'm in breach of contract," Luc began, his voice faltering ever so slightly.

Elise's eyebrows shot up. "You're what?"

Nervously, he reached for a paper in the back pocket of his pants and pulled it out, pointing to a clause in their sales contract. "Since you won't be receiving any commission on the property," he said.

Elise shook her head. "That was just with a sale," she told him. Surely, he hadn't flown out all that way for that reason. Besides, it didn't take an expert to figure that out.

Luc persisted, shoving the paper back in his pocket. "Okay, but I still brought you out all that way to Marseille for nothing," he said, his look pleading.

Elise cocked her head to one side, a slow smile forming. "I wouldn't say it was for *nothing*."

Luc began to smile too, before he blurted out. "I did the calculations. More or less, the commission that you would have gotten for my property in Marseille was around what I paid for the Dalmation street estate." Was he saying what she thought he was saying? He pulled out a set of keys and placed them firmly in her hand. "Take it."

Elise shook her head incredulously. "I can't..." she faltered.

Luc was having none of it. "Elise, take it."

There was a moment of silence between them, as Elise registered what was happening. She nodded, an overwhelming feeling of relief washing over her. Luc was there. She finally had her house back. She didn't know what to make of it all.

Finally, she felt collected enough to speak. "You didn't come out all this way to give me a set of keys, did you?" she asked, hoping that he hadn't.

Luc shook his head, taking one step closer to her. "You said that the distance between us was too far apart. That it wasn't feasible," Luc began, clearing his throat nervously. "Well, I wanted to tell you that the distance isn't too bad. Especially if you catch a red-eye..." Elise took him in. His eyes were searching and frantic, looking at her face for any sign of if she reciprocated his feelings. "You told me you thought I needed to take time to care for myself. You're the first person who has really cared like that."

Elise was touched. Her pulse radiated through her entire body. The entire world around him blurred at the edges.

"The truth is," Luc continued, not taking his eyes off of hers. "I took your advice. I took some time for myself, I've begun connecting again with Annette, and you were right about Marliane," he said, frowning. "She's great. Creative. I asked her if she would be interested in taking a position at Dubonier Entreprises, which she declined, but she's now taking a course to be a florist part-time," he said, frowning. "And then once all of those things started aligning, I realized there was one part of my life that felt completely off-course."

Elise's mouth felt dry, and she swallowed the lump in her throat. "What's that?" she asked.

"I've never felt more misdirected as I did when you left," he said, a slow smile forming in the corner of his mouth. Elise smiled back, inching closer to him. He raised his hand to meet hers, a warm feeling swelling up in her chest. "Plus, Joie misses you," he added teasingly. Elise couldn't help but laugh. "Now, at the risk of being rejected twice, can I kiss you?" he asked softly.

And just like that, Elise stepped forward and kissed the Marseille millionaire.

Chapter Twenty-Four

Two Months Later

The walls of Raising Rose were packed high with knick-knacks. Or as Rose called it all, *inventory*.

"Seriously, people wear this?" Elise asked, holding up a granny-style lace shawl.

Rose grabbed it from her. "Careful! That one has already sold online. I'm just waiting for them to come pick it up."

Elise had to hand it to her sister–she had done *well*. Her Instagram-based vintage shop had been such a hit she was now opening up her very own stand-alone location of Raising Rose. So far, there was still a lot of work to be done. But Elise took one look at her sister, determinedly folding and tagging items, and knew she didn't have a thing to worry about.

"Where can I put this?" Luc walked in from the truck, arms filled high with neon pink jumpsuits.

Rose's face lit up. "Over here!" she said, standing and making room on a rolling clothes rack. "These are some brand-new items that I'll be selling," she said, stroking the silky fabric. "So the standalone shop will offer something a little unique. Vintage *and* brand-new items."

Luc nodded and began clearing away some empty paint cans along the edges of the shop. Elise beamed, looking at Luc helping in her sister's new shop. For the last two months, the pair of them had been inseparable. Luc claimed that staying in Ashfield was best for business, since he was doing research into expanding Dubonier Entreprises into the American market, and had been staying at her new Dalmatian Street address.

She couldn't deny it–it had been the most fantastic relief to walk back into that house and know that it was *hers*. And waking up in that familiar home with Luc next to her and Langdon curled up at her feet... that had to be the best feeling in the world.

Although they had spent the last month back in Marseille, where she had put even more homey-touches into his house, including commissioning a wall-sized painting from Mario himself of the Old Port. It had been his masterpiece, Mario had told them, as they had it hung and photographed for his new website, which Jacques had helped him with. She felt like between Ashfield and Marseille, she had two very strong, warm networks of a new extended family. It warmed her to the core at the thought.

They had only arrived back in Ashfield earlier that morning, with Joie in tow. When back in Marseille, she had once again teamed up with Jacques–this time to find Alex and Clara a home in Marseille. But they had settled on a six-bedroom harbor-view apartment in the heart of the city which after many conversations about their needs, turned out to be exactly what they had wanted.

Elise's attention was brought back to Raising Rose as she continued to fold. Joie ran around the new office space, sniffing new corners and nudging piles of clothing before curling up on a pile of sweaters. Rose had chosen a delicate champagne-pink color for the walls, with little gold rose vines painted along the edges she had done herself. Although Elise had been certain it would look campy, up close it looked well, *stunning*.

Rose turned on her old-fashioned record player, complete with a brass horn. On it, she put a record of some bluesy music. It was one of those moments where everything felt right in the world. After all that they had been through, Elise looked at Rose who was happily humming along to the music, and knew that everything would be fine.

Elise was continuing to rummage through piles of clothing when Luc walked over to her. "Check your purse," he suggested, holding out Lord to her. He handed it to Elise. Curiously, she opened it. Inside was a black box. Her heart pounded as her gaze shot up at Luc. Misty eyed, he nodded. She turned the box over in her hands. It was obviously an antique box, with delicate carvings throughout. "Open it," he urged her. Joie let out a high-pitched bark in excitement.

Elise looked up from the box to see Luc staring at her, his eyes suddenly glassy. She turned to Rose, who already had tears streaming down her face, and was doing her best to suppress them. She turned back to Luc, her heart now racing and she could feel the blood rushing to her cheeks.

She opened up the box carefully and drew a deep breath. Inside the box was the most perfect solitaire diamond set on a gold band. It sparkled in the sunlight, streaming through the windows. With wide eyes, she turned back to Luc. She could feel her pulse radiating through her entire body. Emotion swelled up in her in a way she had never felt.

"Elise, will you–" Luc began, reaching out to hold her hand.

"—But what about Rose!" Elise suddenly blurted out, before she could stop herself. "We can't move to Marseille and leave Rose!"

Now it was Rose's turn to jump in. "Elise, Luc has a house here. With you. Remember? And in case you hadn't figured it out yet, I'm actually fairly self-sufficient," she said enthusiastically. Elise looked from Rose, who nodded at her, and back to Luc–a calm, patient look on his face.

"At risk of sounding like an idiot," he said with a laugh, now bending onto one knee. "I'll try one more time," he said with a wink. "Elise, will you marry me?"

Elise's head was spinning. Tears sprung from her eyes as she clasped her hands around the back of his neck and pulled him close. There was only one answer. One perfect response.

"*Oui*!"

The End

Acknowledgements

I'd like to thank my wonderful family and friends for your support. A special thanks to Pumpkin and Jagger, who kept me company the entire time I wrote. Finally, a huge *merci* to the citizens of Marseille who made me feel entirely at home in your city.

About the Author

KAYA QUINSEY HOLT IS the author of *The Marseille Millionaire*, as well as the books *Paris Mends Broken Hearts, Valentine in Venice,* and *A Coastal Christmas.* Marseille was the first stop on her honeymoon. She lives in Toronto with her husband.

www.kayaquinsey.com
www.goodreads.com/kayaquinsey
Twitter: @KayaQuinseyHolt
Instagram: @KayaQuinseyHolt

Turn the page for an exciting peak into Kaya's upcoming book, **Fate at the Wisteria Estate (The Pink Shell Shores Book #1).** Available February 28, 2020.

Sneak Peak: Fate at the Wisteria Estate (The Pink Shell Shores Series Book #1)

The New Year always brought out the best intentions in people. At least, according to Aribella "Bell" Lacroix. That's why she had moved to Pink Shell Shores a few days before. She had celebrated the New Year's countdown surrounded by boxes at varying stages of unpacking. Located at 14 Oyster Lane, Bell's new seaside cottage was coming along. Within the few days she had been there, she had unpacked twenty-six boxes. There had been three rounds of tears, a bottle of cabernet sauvignon, and endless calls to Lacey Lacroix–her identical twin-sister. Now, Bell was almost completely unpacked.

"What do you think, Georgia?"

Georgia Lacroix, the ancient one-eyed English Toy Spaniel glanced up at her from her plush bed. Bell had rescued her from the animal shelter a few years earlier. Georgia resumed licking herself.

Bell smiled and looked around the living room. "It's perfect."

The putty colored walls of her two-bedroom, three-bathroom bungalow already had photos of her and Lacey from their childhood, pictures of her parents in their post-retirement Florida house, and the medley of artwork she had collected from her travels in the Mediterranean all of those summers ago...

As if on cue, her iPhone began to ring.

"I'm done!" Bell pronounced the second she had pressed reply.

In the background was the familiar sound of her twin nieces, Presley and Olivia. They were fighting over something, which made for loud and distracting noise.

"Like, *everything*?" Lacey asked, louder than usual to be heard over the commotion. Lacey didn't sound convinced. Bell couldn't blame her. It had taken Bell over a year to settle into her last apartment outside of Boston. A few weeks earlier, while she had been packing to move to Pink Shell Shores, Bell had even found a couple of still-packed boxes in the back of a closet. She couldn't bring herself to tell Lacey about them.

"I know you don't believe me. But that's why you, Gunner, and the girls have to come visit me in a few weeks. Seriously, Lace–I have a guest room for you and Gunner, and the girls won't mind a blow up mattress. It's–it's a different world down here."

Bell looked around her new home with wide eyes, still barely believing that this was now her reality. A shiver of excitement ran down her spine. She thought back to the first moment she laid eyes on Pink Shell Shores only a few days before. A few weeks earlier, Bell had accepted a new job. A prestigious job. Just thinking about it created butterflies.

She had accepted and signed a contract as a wedding and venue coordinator at the Wisteria Estate. It was a renowned venue for weddings and high-end boutique hotel. Located smack dab in the middle of Pink Shell Shores in North Carolina. She had been so excited; she accepted immediately without so much as having been near the small coastal town. She had been ready for a change. Scratch that–she was *desperate*.

Within the past month, Nigel McLeary (her ex-boyfriend of *many* years) had gotten married. Just thinking about it made her stomach churn. As if that wasn't bad enough, it was to a girl he had known for only six months. It didn't help matters much that Nigel was also the manager of The Saint Thomas Hotel. It was also where Bell had worked as a wedding and venue coordinator for the last five years. To make matters worse, The Saint Thomas (as staff called it) was flooded with memories. Where Nigel had first asked her out. Their first kiss. That room where they had first... Plus, the buddy-buddy persona that Nigel had tried to cultivate with her since their breakup seemed phony on the best days. It was patronizing at the worst. It got to be too much.

As if the universe was trying to give her more of a giant nudge to get out of The Saint Thomas, her apartment complex had caught fire. No one was hurt. Luckily, Georgia had been with her dog walker at the time. Later, the residents of the apartment were told it would be another two months or so before they were allowed to move back in. There were structural repairs that needed to be taken care of. Bell had barely enough time between applying to the job at the Wisteria Estate, getting accepted, and packing up her boxes to say goodbye to Lacey, Gunner, and the girls.

Now, as she paced in the living room of her cozy house in Pink Shell Shores, it felt like ages ago that she piled her mint-green Volkswagen with moving boxes and set off on the eleven-hour road trip from Boston to Pink Shell Shores. The agricultural land and highways had eventually given way to Carolinian forests, pastel-colored shingled houses, and old colonial manors. As Bell drove into her new town, Pink Shell Shores had made her think if Nantucket and Charleston had a baby town, and then shrunk it...

Lacey's voice snapped Bell back to the present moment. "You know we'd all love to come down and visit, Bell, but the girls just started first grade and we don't want to disrupt their routine or anything."

After a brief jolt, Bell agreed with her sister. It still surprised her whenever she heard how old the twins–the *new* set of twins–were getting. Lacey having twins was a shock given that everyone loves a twin-who-is-having-twins story. But, the real surprise to Bell and their parents had been that Lacey was 21-years-old when she and Gunner got pregnant. To everyone's amazement, Gunner had cleaned up his party-boy ways right away. He had proposed, and they had a small wedding ceremony for their respective immediate families. Thinking about back when Gunner used to pound tequila four nights a week made Bell stifle a giggle. He used to know the bouncers to the best clubs in Boston. Now, Bell couldn't think of a more responsible man. He was a partner at an insurance brokerage. He and Lacey were members at an exclusive member-only tennis club. He drank red wine and spoiled his kids at Christmas.

"Plus, Gunner's been really busy at work," Lacey added with a touch of pride.

"Amazing!" she said with a little too much punctuation.

Bell always forced a little excitement into her tone whenever her sister talked about Gunner. There was one quirk of his that drove her nuts. He had this way of remembering *everything*. Especially embarrassing facts said in a moment of letting her guard down. And he often brought them up again at unsavory moments. Not maliciously, but in a way that made Bell wonder if his parents had skipped the lesson on tact.

You've gotten into an accident before and were deemed at fault, right Bell?

You cry every time you hear The Cranberries, right Bell?

You used to read wedding magazines and pretend you were getting married, right Bell?

You've been a bridesmaid four times now, right Bell?

You haven't had any other serious relationships other than Nigel, right Bell?

Changing the subject, Bell brought up the one topic she knew Lacey was sure to bring up anyway. She took a deep breath, psyching herself up.

"Well, the dating pool in Pink Shell Shores sure looks slim."

Bell had already looked through at the dating app on her phone, swiping through the photos and description of potential matches in the area. One of them had a fantastic picture of himself at the beach, but that was before she read on his bio that he was also into nun chucks. Another seemed very transparent that he wasn't looking for something serious. She shuddered thinking about the other potential match–a man who had a list of deal breakers including 'women who cry during movies'. What was wrong with that?

Bell had moved to Pink Shell Shores for her job. *Not* to fall in love.

Visit Kaya Quinsey Holt's website at

www.kayaquinsey.com

Made in United States
North Haven, CT
06 December 2022

28079260R00098